Christian Recovery

A TWELVE-STEP APPROACH
TO DISCIPLESHIP

PROVIDENCE

AUSTIN ✚ TEXAS

· SOLI DEO GLORIA ·

CONTENTS

PREFACE

"The time is fulfilled, and the kingdom of God is at hand; repent and believe in the gospel."

MARK 1:15

When someone comes to us asking for help with sin and pain, our suggestion is simple: "Get a sponsor, work the steps."

Why? This simple formula has changed our lives, and it can change yours.

Most of us were trapped in destructive cycles of sin. Some of us struggled with substance abuse, others with sexual addiction and lust, still others with control, anxiety, anger, or codependency. Many struggled with all the above and others.

But by working the steps, our eyes were opened. We discovered that the path of contentment and joy was through submission to God, not the false promises of sin. We took on Jesus's yoke, discovered it was easy, and found rest for our troubled souls (Matthew 11:28-30).

In our experience, the steps are a simple yet comprehensive way to rigorously apply Jesus's core teachings about powerlessness, humility, dependence on God, confession, prayer, reconciliation, and service to others. The steps are a way of saying, "I don't know how to fix your problem, but God does. Seek him first and these other things will be added to you."

Put differently, the steps don't replace or add to the gospel of Jesus Christ (as if such a thing were possible). Instead, the steps help us apply it to all areas of our lives. And by doing so, we are building on his sure foundation, that will help us withstand the storms of life.

And what is a sponsor? A sponsor is someone who has worked the steps before and can show you how to do the same.

They're not necessarily more spiritually mature, but they've walked the road before and can help you do the same. A sponsor is like a guide to the steps. They don't advise or counsel. They simply show you how they walked the road, help carry your burden, and then help hold you accountable to keep moving.

Is it possible to work the steps without a sponsor? With God, all things are possible. But we have never seen it done successfully. In our experience, sponsors are an indispensable part of all 12-step programs. Without a sponsor, you are not really working a 12-step program as described in this book.

So where does this book fit in? This book was written as an instruction manual to help you work the steps with your sponsor. Specifically, it was designed to be read aloud and discussed together, step by step, and then applied exactly.

Three warnings before we begin.

First, Christian Recovery is not a replacement for other 12-step programs. We've created this program because we've found it helpful for Christians in recovery to have a shared framework for encouragement, exhortation, and accountability based on the teachings of Jesus Christ. But we encourage you to seek out fellow-sufferers in other recovery programs geared towards your particular struggles.

Second, this book is not a guide to becoming a Christian in twelve easy steps. As Christians, we believe there is nothing we must or even can do to make ourselves right with God (Romans 11:6). **We are made right with God by grace through faith in his Son Jesus Christ, not by works or by the 12 steps** (Ephesians 2:8-9). We assume that our readers are already believers, and therefore have already been made right with God through the righteousness of Christ. If that doesn't describe you yet, this book may not be a helpful place to begin your inquiry.

Third, this book is an instruction manual. If you want to get the results that we've got, you must do the things we've done. Please do not think that by attending a few meetings or reading this book that you'll "get better." You must be a doer of the word, and not a hearer only. Christian Recovery is a program for believers to become more spiritually fit.[1] And we achieve spiritual fitness in the same way athletes achieve physical fitness: through training, not by reading books about training. Therefore, action—and lots of it—is necessary.

With that said, let's begin our work.

---

[1] *Cf.* 1 Corinthians 9:24-27.

INTRODUCTION

"Sirs, what must I do to be saved?" And they said, "Believe in the Lord Jesus, and you will be saved, you and your household." And they spoke the word of the Lord to him and to all who were in his house.

ACTS 16:30-32

The Bible appears to say very little about recovery from addiction and compulsive behavior. But, as the saying goes, appearances can be deceiving.

In biblical Greek, the word "saved," like our English word "saved," is synonymous with deliver, protect, rescue, or heal. We typically view Christ's offer of salvation as nothing more than an offer of legal acquittal (*i.e.*, saved from God's wrath). Certainly, to be saved is not less than legal acquittal (Romans 5:9), but it is also so much more. Our salvation in Christ encompasses physical and spiritual renewal and healing, adoption into God's family, entitlement to a spiritual inheritance, and the restoration of a loving relationship with our creator.

In other words, "salvation" is a big word. So, it helps to clarify terms. In biblical usage, the term "salvation" includes our past salvation ("We have been saved") already accomplished by Christ's finished work on the cross, our present salvation ("We are being saved") now being accomplished by the Holy Spirit at work in us to remake us more and more in Christ's image, and our future salvation ("We will be saved") to be accomplished by Christ when he returns in glory. In this present book, we focus primarily on the present tense usage, the daily struggle against sin in our lives, also known as "sanctification." We have been saved and one day we will be saved, but for now we must focus on being saved, day-by-day, through the Holy Spirit.

So, when we ask, "How do I recover?" we are really asking, "What must I do to be saved?" and, more particularly, "What must I do to be saved (sanctified) from the power of sin?" This question, obviously, is one that the Bible answers repeatedly, and one that this book will address in detail.

But first, we must lay the proper foundation. Before we can address our present salvation, we must first address our past salvation, also known as our "justification."

To be "justified" typically means to be "declared righteous" or "shown righteous," particularly in a forensic sense, as for example by a judge. It is used predominantly by the Apostle Paul as a technical term to describe God's act of removing the guilt of sin and crediting Christ's perfect righteousness to those who are united with Christ through faith. To be justified is to be declared righteous by God because of Christ's work on your behalf.

"Justification" occurs by grace alone through faith alone in Christ alone, apart from any of our good works or sincere efforts (Ephesians 2:8-9). It is a gift of God, received by *anyone* who believes in Jesus Christ (John 3:16). Aside from believing in his Son, there is nothing we need to do or even can do to "get right" with God. Nor is there anything else we need to do to "stay right" with God. Once we have been united with Christ by faith, we are free of any threat of condemnation (Romans 8:1). Once we are justified, we are reconciled and have peace with God. This reconciliation and peace, in turn, lays the groundwork for the rest of our salvation (Romans 5:1, 9-11). There is no sanctification unless there is first justification.

It is hard to overstress the importance of justification. Because we are unholy, we are naturally afraid to draw near to a holy God (Genesis 3:10). But since we have been justified by Christ's death and resurrection, we have peace with God. As a result, we can now draw near to him with confidence, not based on our own merits, but on the merits of Christ, our High Priest (Hebrews 4:16).

Having explained this distinction between justification and sanctification, we can now proceed to answer the question posed by the Philippian jailer in its fullest sense: "What must I do to be saved?"

"Believe in the Lord Jesus, and you will be saved!" is the Apostle Paul's response to that question. But what does this mean, and how does that relate to recovery? A full response is not possible in this short text. For now, we wish to offer an overview of the problem and an overview of the solution. This can be summarized in five basic points, borrowing loosely from the Apostle Paul's sermon to the Areopagus.[2]

First, we all intuitively feel a pull towards an "unknown god" who created and ordered the world and everything in it, and who gave us a longing to seek him, find him, and have peace with him. In other words, humans have an inherent drive to worship God.

Second, this longing has been tragically distorted. Our worship-instinct has been tainted by our unwillingness to acknowledge God. Because we know that "unknown god" is wholly good and righteous and we are not, we all naturally suppress the truth about him and try to satisfy our innate drive to worship God by replacing him with lesser things, such as possessions, success, family, prosperity, comfort, drugs, partying, or sex. These idols, in turn, lure us further down the path of unrighteousness and slavery to sin. Contrary to our design, we end up worshiping

---

[2] See Acts 17.

created things rather than the creator. In other words, we all suffer from a worship disorder that is destroying us.

Third, while this "unknown god" has long overlooked our spiritual adultery in hopes that we would turn back to him, he has fixed a day on which he will judge the world in righteousness. Our idolatry will come into the light, and we will be without excuse when the secrets of our hearts are exposed.

Fourth, this "unknown god" has revealed himself through his son, Jesus of Nazareth, promised by ancient prophets, born of a woman, anointed by God's Holy Spirit, filled with power to heal and restore, rejected by men, crucified for the sins of his people, raised from the dead before many witnesses, ascended into heaven, and appointed to one day return to judge the living and the dead.

Lastly, this God now commands us to turn back to him and offers amnesty on simple terms: Anyone who believes in Jesus of Nazareth will be saved—spared from his judgment, reconciled with God, freed from the bondage of the idols that ensnare our hearts—and will receive true and everlasting life, full communion with God, and the satisfaction of all those longings that go unmet by pursuing these false gods. But those who refuse to believe will receive the due penalty of their error, separation from God, who is the ultimate source of fulfillment and satisfaction.

In short, our addictive and compulsive behaviors are the manifestation of a worship disorder. We are made with a spiritual thirst for God. We cannot will this away any more than we can will away our physical thirst. When we turn our backs on him, we turn to other things to slake our thirst: drugs and alcohol, sexual fulfillment, careerism, money, gambling, love, affirmation, and so forth. But these things, even the good ones, cannot replace God. They are dry and empty wells. They give us just enough fulfillment that we keep coming back for more, but they never truly satisfy us. The more we rely on these empty wells, the thirstier we become, and the thirstier we get, the more desperate and frantic our efforts to find water become. Sometimes we try to declare our independence from these dry wells, and strike out in search of other water. Sometimes we find other wells, which are themselves dry. More often, though, we simply give up and return to the well we know. Either way, the result is the same: we sit huddled over empty wells clawing away at the ground in a futile effort to extract whatever water we can until we finally succumb to our thirst and die.

The real outrage is that this miserable situation is entirely unnecessary. The world may offer only empty and dry wells, but God offers a fountain of living water (Jeremiah 2:13; John 7:38). Yet we would rather die of thirst in the wilderness than leave our idols and turn to God.

The solution, then, is clear: return to God, the fountain of living water. He offers us lasting satisfaction where our compulsive behaviors offered only fleeting contentment. This is not a quick and easy process. It is a task we must undertake each day for the rest of our lives. Years of spiritual thirst have caused lasting damage to our hearts and our willpower. But the good news is this: With God, all things are possible (Mark 10:27). God loved us enough to give up Christ his Son for us while we were still enemies, dead in our sins. Now that we are his children, granted spiritual life, how will he not also with Christ graciously give us all things (Romans 8:31)?

God makes extravagant promises to his children. He will set us free from our bondage and cleanse us of our sins (1 John 1:9). He will aid us in overcoming temptation (1 Corinthians 10:13). He will fill our hearts with good fruit (Galatians 5:22-23) and lavish us with his good gifts (Ezekiel 36:25-27). He will supply all our needs (Philippians 4:19) and begin to renew our minds (Romans 12:2). He will fill us with his wisdom (James 1:5) and give us his peace. (John 14:27). In short, he will do for us those things that we cannot do for ourselves.

OUR PROCESS

Before we begin, here is a brief outline of the process described in this book:

Step One: Powerlessness
We acknowledged our powerlessness over sin and the destructive effect it had on our lives.

Step Two: Hope
We recognized that, by putting our hope in the restorative love of God through Jesus Christ, we could find healing and victory over our sinful tendencies.

Step Three: Surrender
We surrendered all aspects of our lives over to the care and direction of God, seeking to serve his will.

Step Four: Self-Examination
We made a thorough examination of ourselves by preparing a moral inventory.

Step Five: Confession
We shared our inventory with another person in order to confess the depths of our sin and brokenness.

Step Six: Commitment
We committed to growing in holiness.

Step Seven: Grace
We pursued holiness by humbly relying upon God's transforming work in our hearts and petitioning him for renewal.

Step Eight: Forgiveness
We considered all people we had harmed and sought to forgive them.

Step Nine: Reconciliation
We attempted reconciliation with such people by making direct amends for any wrongs we had committed.

Step Ten: Mortification
We sought to put off the old self through continued use of the inventory process.

Step Eleven: Prayer and Meditation
We sought to put on the new self through a regular process of prayer and meditation.

Step Twelve: Sponsorship
We shared our experiences with others hoping to recover and led them through this process via sponsorship.

We encourage you to reference this process with your sponsor as you work your way through the book together.

STEP ONE
POWERLESSNESS

For the wrath of God is revealed from heaven against all ungodliness and unrighteousness of men, who by their unrighteousness suppress the truth. For what can be known about God is plain to them, because God has shown it to them. For his invisible attributes, namely, his eternal power and divine nature, have been clearly perceived, ever since the creation of the world, in the things that have been made. So they are without excuse. For although they knew God, they did not honor him as God or give thanks to him, but they became futile in their thinking, and their foolish hearts were darkened. Claiming to be wise, they became fools, and exchanged the glory of the immortal God for images resembling mortal man and birds and animals and creeping things.

* * * *

And since they did not see fit to acknowledge God, God gave them up to a debased mind to do what ought not to be done. They were filled with all manner of unrighteousness, evil, covetousness, malice. They are full of envy, murder, strife, deceit, maliciousness. They are gossips, slanderers, haters of God, insolent, haughty, boastful, inventors of evil, disobedient to parents, foolish, faithless, heartless, ruthless. Though they know God's righteous decree that those who practice such things deserve to die, they not only do them but give approval to those who practice them.

ROMANS 1:18-23, 28-31

Understanding compulsive sin requires understanding three truths.

First, sin is the result of a worship disorder. We have exchanged the glory of the immortal God for lesser passions, and as a result, we slip deeper into our passions. The result is sin: impurity and lusts, sexual immorality, and "all manner of unrighteousness." Our covetousness—the twisted and insatiable desires—is not merely tantamount to idolatry, but also the result of it.

Second, sin is progressively enslaving. Idolatry begets more idolatry, and sin begets more sin (James 1:14-15). The more we sin, the easier it becomes to sin again, and the more we become controlled by it (Romans 6:16). Sin *promises* freedom, but *results in* slavery.

Third, sin's slavery is subtle and deceptive. People who think they are free are the ones who are most enslaved:

So Jesus said to the Jews who had believed him, "If you abide in my word, you are truly my disciples, and you will know the truth, and the truth will set you free." They answered him, "We are offspring of Abraham and have never been enslaved to anyone.

How is it that you say, 'You will become free'?"

Jesus answered them, "Truly, truly, I say to you, everyone who practices sin is a slave to sin. The slave does not remain in the house forever; the son remains forever. So if the Son sets you free, you will be free indeed. I know that you are offspring of Abraham; yet you seek to kill me because my word finds no place in you. I speak of what I have seen with my Father, and you do what you have heard from your father."

JOHN 8:31-38

In the above passage, Christ delivers his iconic promise: "You will know the truth, and the truth will set you free." He offers his hearers spiritual freedom, and they reject his offer of freedom because they cannot comprehend the fact that they might be spiritual slaves. This passage points to the hopelessness of our condition apart from Christ. Sin is our master and we don't even realize it because we love to do what our master tells us to do, so we never need to be coerced.

Understanding these three truths—(1) that all sin is the result of idolatry, (2) that sin is progressively enslaving, and (3) that sin deludes us into believing we are "free"—is not just the key to understanding compulsive sin, but also its remedy.

Because we misunderstood the nature of our problem, our attempts to solve the problem failed.

Firstly, because we misunderstood the root cause of sin (idolatry), we wasted years, sometimes decades, of our lives trying to control our behavior. We tried to moderate our drinking, only to get drunk the next day. We tried to end our dysfunctional relationship one week, only to return to it the next. We installed anti-pornographic software on our computer, only to circumvent it later that night.

We were focused on the behavior (sinful actions), not the root cause (idolatry). Yes, it is good to struggle against our sinful actions. But if we fail to address the underlying idolatry, we will never experience lasting freedom. We were imposing on ourselves elemental regulations, regulations that seemed helpful, but in reality, were useless in stopping the indulgence of our sinful desires (Colossians 2:20-23).

Secondly, because we misunderstood the nature of sin (that it is progressively enslaving), we succumbed to the lie that we could weaken our sin by giving into temptation. Yet the seductive power of sin, particularly addictive sin, is that yielding to temptation on one occasion makes it more difficult to resist temptation on the next. In other words, we reap what we sow (Galatians 6:7-8). We found that when we sowed the seed of sin, we reaped a harvest of sinful behavior. When we gratified the desires of our sinful flesh,[3] we not only increased its power over us, we also choked

---

[3] In biblical usage, the term "flesh" usually denotes the "natural" (*i.e.*, fallen) aspects of human nature, body, and soul. *Cf.* John 1:13 ("will of the flesh").

out the power of the Spirit (Galatians 5:16-17). We often told ourselves things like, "I'll just have one drink tonight and get back on the wagon tomorrow," only to find that by the next day we had lost our will to fight. This principle holds true for any sinful behavior. We are either killing our sin or our sin is killing us (Romans 8:13).

Thirdly, because we misunderstood the nature of our estate (that we were slaves to sin), we were unable to fully comprehend sin's power over us. Before we recovered, most of us were unwilling to admit our captivity. We didn't like to think of ourselves as slaves. Instead, we told ourselves that we chose to drink because we liked it or we chose to watch pornography because we wanted to. Unquestionably this was true—we did love to drink and we did want to watch pornography—but this was only half of the truth. The other half of the truth is that we couldn't have stopped if we wanted to. Because we loved indulging in our sin so much, we were rarely confronted with our inability to stop, and so we persisted in the delusion that we were in control of our behavior.

On their own, apart from God, these efforts tended to fail because we lacked the power to bring about the change we sought. The full extent of our spiritual slavery became apparent only after we tried to escape from the bondage of sin and failed, sometimes repeatedly. Sin was our master. Sometimes sweetly, sometimes harshly, it controlled every aspect of our lives, and always managed to prevent our escape. We were powerless to resist it.

In the end, we began to realize that our false gods would not—could not—save us. We turned to these false gods in a desperate attempt to control our lives, but in the end these false gods controlled us. We had to admit that our attempts to control our lives were a failure, and by the time we discovered this sad truth, it was already too late for us to escape on our own power.

The above can be summarized like this: In order to be free from the compulsive power of our compulsive sins, we needed to abstain completely, and yet any attempt to moderate, control, or abstain from destructive behavior was doomed to failure. This is the horrible nature of spiritual slavery, and no amount of self-help, self-knowledge, or self-will can liberate us.

As Christians, we know this isn't the end of the story. We were at one time slaves to sin and enemies of God, but now through Christ we have received freedom and been adopted by God.

But it doesn't always feel that way. We too struggle with these same problems, doing things we didn't really want to do and still feeling as if we were "sold under sin" (Romans 7:13-20).

Here, we think we were fooling ourselves as to the extent of our problem. Being freed *from* sin and free *of* sin are two very different things. We now had the power and desire to resist sin, but the lingering effects of our slavery to sin continued with us (Romans 8:15). Our hearts, shaped by years of habitual sin, continued to be "deceitful above all things" and continued to seek satisfaction in things that were not God. We may be free from sin in our inner being, but sin continues to dwell in our corrupted body (Romans 7:21-25).

If we hope that a few meetings and a little honesty will yield a quick victory over sin, we misunderstand the nature of the problem. The struggle against sin—generally and particularly—is a life-long struggle. Nowhere does Christ promise us a simple and self-directed victory over sin ("I'll set you free, and then you can take it from there!"). Instead, we are in constant need of his continuing grace, and the more grace we receive, the more we realize we need it. Nothing good dwells in our flesh, and we lack even the power to carry out the good things we desire to do (Romans 8:18).

Christ explains the extent of our powerlessness, even as believers, in the Upper Room Discourse. He tells us that he is the vine and we are the branches, and that therefore apart from him we can do nothing (John 15:4-5). Note: it is not just that we are powerless over alcohol, drugs, pornography, dysfunctional relationships, or sexual behavior. Rather, there is not one single thing we can do without Christ. Without his help, all our best plans and efforts will come to nothing (Psalm 127:1).

So, the first step in recovery is not just recognizing that we have a problem. Nor is it even recognizing that we have a problem that will require a lifetime to fix. Rather, the first step in recovery is recognizing the problem and acknowledging that we cannot fix our "problem"—or anything else—without God's help.

STEP ONE PRACTICAL APPLICATION

As we prepare to begin this process, there are three practical steps we can take: (1) admitting our weakness, (2) working with a sponsor, and (3) seeking out community.

Admitting Our Weakness. We accept that we lack the power to break free of sin without God's help: apart from him, we can do nothing. So, long as we rely on our own strength, we will never be free from the power of sin.

So, we must ask ourselves: "Do I admit that I am powerless over my sin, and that my life is unmanageable?" If we struggle with this truth, we have found it helpful to put pen to paper, writing down examples where we are powerless over our behavior (doing things we know we shouldn't or not doing things we know we should) and where our lives have become unmanageable (areas where we have not been able to manage the circumstances in our lives to our satisfaction).

Working with a Sponsor. By now, we should be working with a sponsor and humbly taking direction. Having a sponsor is a practical acknowledgment that we need help. It is also a good practice. Experience shows that without another experienced person to guide us and hold us accountable, we tend to seek out the easier, softer way to manage our sin, rather than turning to God and letting him change us.

Seek Out Fellowship. Recognizing that God will work on you through people, we should begin to seek out fellowship. In particular, start going to twelve-step meetings or, if no meetings are available, something similar (accountability groups, small groups, etc.). If you need help finding suitable meetings, ask your sponsor or a pastor to point you in the right direction. We have found it necessary to fully immerse ourselves in this new fellowship and new way of life. We have found that checking in once a week is simply not enough, at least early on, and so we recommend trying to make several meetings every week. Some even find it helpful to make several a day. In other words, the more, the better.

Moreover, fellowship is a two-way street. To the extent we are benefiting from the fellowship of others, we should in turn be ready to extend the hand of fellowship to another person in need. No matter how new or bad off we are, there's always someone newer or worse off that we can try to help.

STEP TWO
HOPE

If then you have been raised with Christ, seek the things that are above, where Christ is, seated at the right hand of God. Set your minds on things that are above, not on things that are on earth. For you have died, and your life is hidden with Christ in God. When Christ who is your life appears, then also you will appear with him in glory.

COLOSSIANS 3:1-4

By grace through faith in Jesus Christ we can overcome our sin and recover from our addictions. The God who spoke the world into existence, who continues to uphold it by the power of his word, and who meticulously cares for us right down to the hairs on our heads, makes that possible. It is absurd to think that he cannot free us (Jeremiah 32:17, 27).

It is equally absurd to think that he will not free us. God loves us more than we love ourselves, and more than we can even comprehend (Ephesians 3:18). In fact, his love for us is so strong that he sent his son to die for us while we were still sinners (Romans 5:6-10). Now that we have been redeemed, nothing can separate us from that love (Romans 8:35-39). We are his children, and he is eager to bestow his best gifts upon us. Indeed, God is working all things together for our good (Romans 8:28). Through his grace, we can find freedom from our addictions. Our experience has proven that in countless cases.

Yet, if we are honest, here we run into a problem. Many of us have tried (time and again) to overcome our sin. We have prayed, invited others into our struggles, confessed our sins, practiced abstinence, studied his word, and struggled against the desires of our flesh. Yet we never experienced freedom or that freedom was short-lived. We felt as though God may be helping others with their struggles, but he was not helping us.

Our problem, we think, was that we were zealous, but not according to knowledge (Romans 10:2). The Bible is shot through with promises of spiritual freedom. Yet God grants this freedom in a very particular way:

So Jesus said to the Jews who had believed in him, "If you abide in my word, you are truly my disciples, and you will know the truth, and the truth will set you free."

JOHN 8:31-32

Christ's prescription for freedom is simple: "abide in my word." If you do, you will know the truth, and the truth will set you free. Freedom comes through truth, and truth through abiding in the word of Christ.

So, what is the word of Christ, and how do we abide ("remain") in it? It means three things: (1) to abide in his word about himself, that he is the Christ, the Son of God, and by believing in him we may have life in his name, (2) to abide in his promises, that through faith we might be blessed with all manner of spiritual blessings, and (3) to abide in his commandments, that through obedience to his design for living, we might find joy and contentment and peace in all circumstances. Thus, abiding is first and foremost about believing, and only after that about doing.

First, in the Gospel according to John, the "word" of Christ consists of his teaching about himself: his deity, his value, his beauty, his power, and his life-giving and life-sustaining goodness. He is the all-satisfying bread of life, the life-giving light of the world, the door to the sheepfold of salvation, the good shepherd who lays down his life for his sheep, the resurrection and the life, and the true vine.[4] In other words, to abide in his word is to remain persuaded that he is the Messiah, the Son of God.[5] Indeed, the Gospel according to John was written to emphasize this point, so that "you may believe that Jesus is the Christ, the Son of God, and that by believing you may have life in his name" (John 20:31).

Second, the "word" of Christ consists of his promises, which are attained through faith, not through works. Put differently, to abide in his word is to set our mind on the things that are above, where Christ is, namely the promises of God, which all find their "yes" in him (2 Corinthians 1:20). It is through Christ that these promises are secured for us, and through these promises that we are conformed to the image of Christ. As our mind is renewed, our behavior will follow (Romans 12:2).

Our past attempts at spiritual freedom failed because we misunderstood the nature of spiritual transformation. Having begun our Christian walk by the Spirit through hearing with faith, we attempted to complete our Christian walk on our own willpower, the flesh. The Apostle Paul warns against this:

> *O foolish Galatians! Who has bewitched you? It was before your eyes that Jesus Christ was publicly portrayed as crucified. Let me ask you only this: Did you receive the Spirit by works of the law or by hearing with faith? Are you so foolish? Having begun by the Spirit, are you now being perfected by the flesh? Did you suffer so many things in vain—if indeed it was in vain? Does he who supplies the Spirit to you and works miracles among you do so by works of the law, or by hearing with faith—just as Abraham "believed God, and it was counted to him as righteousness"?*
>
> GALATIANS 3:1-6

---

[4] *Cf.* John 6:35, 8:12, 10:7-8, 10:11, 11:25, 14:6, 15:1.
[5] *Cf.* John 6:53-58.

Paul was correcting the Galatian Christians who (wrongly) believed that there was a second-level Christianity—conversion was by faith, but perfection came through our willpower (the "flesh"). No, says Paul: you are begun by faith, and you are perfected by faith. There is never a time in our Christian walk where we can tell God, "I'll take it from here." Our sanctification always comes by the power of the Spirit through "hearing with faith."

Our problem was that we focused on overcoming our sin (a good thing, to be sure), yet did so to the exclusion of the Spirit. We were undertaking actions that felt godly (prayer, confession, accountability, quiet time), and may even have been good, but doing so wrongly. We were trying to transform ourselves according to our own plans through "self-made religion and asceticism and severity to the body," things that "have indeed the appearance of wisdom" but in reality "are of no value in stopping the indulgence of the flesh" (Colossians 2:23).

Instead, we should have continued as we started: by the Spirit through faith. As we received Christ, so we should walk in him (Colossians 2:6). Rather than focusing all our efforts on combatting our sin, we should focus our efforts primarily on walking by the Spirit. If we do so, then we will not only avoid gratifying the desires of the flesh, we will weaken the power of the flesh, because the Spirit and the flesh are opposed to one another (Galatians 5:16-18).

How do we walk by the Spirit? By faith in Christ, in his promises, in his sufficiency, in his goodness (Colossians 2:6). This absolutely entails putting to death what is sinful in us. But it also entails putting on our new identify—the one Christ Jesus procured for us—which is being renewed after the image of its creator (Colossians 3:10). And this we do by faith, letting the peace of Christ rule our hearts, letting the word of Christ dwell in us richly, and by doing all things "in the name of the Lord Jesus, giving thanks to God the father through him" (Colossians 3:15-17).

In short, the task of Christian discipleship begins and ends in the power of the Spirit through faith, setting our minds on the things above where Christ is, treasuring our inheritance in heaven, reveling in God's goodness towards us, and eagerly awaiting the return of Christ Jesus (Colossians 3:1-4).

Third, the "word" of Christ consists of his commandments, namely to love one another:

> *"If you keep my commandments, you will abide in my love, just as I have kept my Father's commandments and abide in his love. These things I have spoken to you, that my joy may be in you, and that your joy may be full. This is my commandment, that you love one another as I have loved you."*
>
> JOHN 15:10-12

When we keep Christ's commandments (which we do by walking in step with the Spirit!), we will abide in his love, and as a result, be filled with joy. Sin's power over us will be weakened by the superior power of Christ's joy! Sin that used to seem tempting will increasingly seem foolish and shortsighted: if we live in the completed joy of Christ, why would we choose the deceptive promises of sin?

The Apostle Paul states this learning so: to be free from sin, we must submit ourselves as slaves to Christ.

> *Do you not know that if you present yourselves to anyone as obedient slaves, you are slaves of the one whom you obey, either of sin, which leads to death, or of obedience, which leads to righteousness? But thanks be to God, that you who were once slaves of sin have become obedient from the heart to the standard of teaching to which you were committed, and, having been set free from sin, have become slaves of righteousness. I am speaking in human terms, because of your natural limitations. For just as you once presented your members as slaves to impurity and to lawlessness leading to more lawlessness, so now present your members as slaves to righteousness leading to sanctification.*
>
> ROMANS 6:16-19

This may seem paradoxical, but freedom from sin comes through slavery to Christ. It is a spiritual axiom that we must serve someone, whether Christ or sin. The only way to break the power of sin, then, is to submit ourselves to Christ as obedient slaves. And in breaking the power of sin, we find peace and joy and contentment in God.

In short, we must trust in Christ, in his work, his promises, and his rule. So, who is this person in whom we should trust? Scripture gives at least six answers:

Jesus is the Son of God. Here, the emphasis is on his divinity. Christ is not simply a great teacher or even a mighty prophet and king anointed by God. He is himself God, worthy of our glory, honor, and worship. All things were created for him and through him, meaning that he is not only the cause of our existence; he is the reason for it.[6]

Jesus is the first of many to be killed and raised. Here, the emphasis is on his humiliation and exaltation. Christ is the God who was mocked, beaten, tortured, and killed, so that he might be Lord of both the living and the dead (Romans 14:9). He willingly humbled himself so that through suffering he might sanctify us and allow us to share with him in his glory.[7]

Jesus is the Great Prophet. Here, the emphasis is on his speaking as a loving, wise, and authoritative God. It is far easier to trust Christ as our savior than to trust him to wisely order our lives, particularly when he bids us to deny ourselves and take up

---

[6] *Cf.* John 20:28-31; 1 John 2:23-25; 1 John 5:13-15.
[7] *Cf.* John 20:28; Romans 10:9; 1 Peter 1:21.

our crosses as his disciples (Mark 8:34). Yet Christ says that his yoke is easy and his burden is light. We are able to keep his commandments because his commands are not burdensome (Matthew 11:30).

Jesus is the Great High Priest. Here, the emphasis is on him not as Lord but as our Savior, whose blood cleanses us from our iniquity and who offers up intercessions for us with God. We naturally slip back into self-righteousness or self-condemnation, rather than resting in his finished work as the only and final way by which men can be reconciled to a holy God.[8]

Jesus is the Great King. Here, the emphasis is on him as the sovereign who can rightfully command obedience. We tend to create the idol of a "Buddy Christ," who loves us and affirms us, but never demands our allegiance. Yes, Jesus is our friend who condescends to us as a supreme act of humility. Yet we exist for his glory, not the other way around, and the Christ who came in humility will come again in glory as judge of the world, and at that time every knee will bow and every tongue will confess that he is Lord (Philippians 2:5-11).

Jesus is the Suffering Servant. Here, the emphasis is on his love and devotion to his people. Christ became the ascendant Lord because he was first the suffering servant. We can get caught up in the power, majesty, and glory of Christ as king and forget that he is particularly our king, who "became the source of eternal salvation to all who obey him through what he suffered" (Hebrews 5:8).

In some ways, the real question is not whether we trust in Christ, but in which "Christ" do we trust. Most spiritual problems can be traced back to lack of believing as we should in his work and his promises. Or, put differently (and as outlined in Step 1), our struggles are rooted in our idolatrous worship, misdirected longings, and misplaced trust.

The solution, therefore, must begin by correcting those problems. Therefore, the approach outlined in this book is designed to turn our hearts, souls, and minds Christward, both in spirit and in practice, and to trust his promises above all else.

STEP TWO PRACTICAL APPLICATION

The practical application for Step 2 is simple. We ask ourselves if we believe, or if we are even willing to believe, that God can and will set us free from our sin. If we can honestly say that we believe, or are at least willing to believe, then we are ready to move forward. If we cannot, then we must turn to God in prayer and ask him to help us in our unbelief.

---

[8] *Cf.* Acts 15:11; Romans 3:24; Hebrews 4:14-16.

STEP THREE
SURRENDER

"Come to me, all who labor and are heavy laden, and I will give you rest. Take my yoke upon you, and learn from me, for I am gentle and lowly in heart, and you will find rest for your souls. For my yoke is easy, and my burden is light."

MATTHEW 11:28-30

Then Jesus told his disciples, "If anyone would come after me, let him deny himself and take up his cross and follow me. For whoever would save his life will lose it, but whoever loses his life for my sake will find it."

MATTHEW 16:24-25

As outlined in Step 2, the path to freedom is trusting in Christ: his work, his promises, and his commands.

Why should this be? The answer begins with the fact that there are two ways to live: our way and God's way.

"Our" way looks different for each of us, but it amounts to this: we choose to do what is right in our own eyes, to live on our own wisdom and for our own glory and benefit.

God's way is the exact opposite: we choose to do what is right in God's eyes, to live on God's wisdom and for God's glory and others' benefit.

Whatever the nature of our sin, the root of our problem is that we are choosing to live life our way, not God's way. We do so because we do not trust God as we should.

Christianity is not merely a means to be reconciled to God, it is a whole design for living. God made us, God loves us, and God knows what's good for us. His commands are not arbitrary. They are at the center of what it means to be a fulfilled human being.

This truth breaks out along two axes: (1) living for ourselves is foolish and unfulfilling, and (2) living for God is the only reliable path to contentment.

Living for our own benefit—self-centeredness, if you will—is flatly counterproductive. We have all learned this truth through bitter experience. The harder we tried to order our affairs to our own liking, the more discontent, unfulfilled, and lonely we felt. We either failed to achieve the desired circumstances, or when we did, it didn't live up to our expectations. When we turn our backs on him and chase after other lovers, we are forsaking the source of true fulfillment, and in the process, condemning ourselves to a life of spiritual thirst:

> *"For my people have committed two evils: they have forsaken me, the fountain of living waters, and hewed out cisterns for themselves, broken cisterns that can hold no water."*
>
> JEREMIAH 2:13

In seeking after false gods—power, control, affirmation, excitement, or comfort—through the priesthood of drugs, alcohol, sex, wealth, ambition, or relationships, we believed we were seeking fulfillment. But sin is deceitful. It promises happiness, but in the end, it delivers only misery and emptiness.

On the other hand, living for God and for others is paradoxically the way of contentment. Jesus famously promised that we will be blessed, be filled with joy, and be content in all circumstances, if we live in the way he tells us to: with his priorities, with his wisdom, with his goals.[9] This state of blessedness includes a sort of happiness: the contentment and fulfillment that comes from God. Put differently, God promises to give you everything you want, but first everything you want is going to change.

In practice, this means our desires need to be reshaped towards God.

Without realizing it, most of us had fallen into the error of believing a gospel of our personal prosperity. We had a vision of what we wanted from life (to be "healthy, wealthy, and wise"), and we expected God to deliver on that vision. Our relationship with God was essentially transactional: we took the actions, we expected God to deliver the results. Therefore, when God did not supply what we wanted (the spouse, the job, the material abundance—or more generally power, respect, comfort, affirmation, and security), we felt discontent and let down by God.

The problem with this way of thinking is that God is not a means to an end. God is the end in himself. He alone is our source of satisfaction. Our hearts are spiritually thirsty, and he is the only source of living water to slake that thirst. As Augustine said, our hearts are made for God, and restless until they find their rest in him. So, until we acknowledge this—that God alone is the source of lasting satisfaction and happiness—we will never experience either.

Most of us needed a deep heart change. We needed to abandon the false gospel of personal prosperity and our transactional view of God. Instead, we must seek after God first, irrespective of the outcome. Like Abraham, we should be willing to

---

[9] *Cf.* Matthew 5:1-11; John 15:11; Philippians 4:11-13.

sacrifice everything to God, and trust that God in his goodness will provide for us. In other words, if we seek first his kingdom and his righteousness, then God in his providence will supply our needs (Matthew 6:33).

Jesus sets these truths out in his Sermon on the Mount.[10] He calls us to think differently, act differently, and feel differently. To the precise extent that we do this, we will be "blessed." To the extent we don't, we are headed for trouble. He summarizes these truths as follows:

> *"Everyone then who hears these words of mine and does them will be like a wise man who built his house on the rock. And the rain fell, and the floods came, and the winds blew and beat on that house, but it did not fall, because it had been founded on the rock. And everyone who hears these words of mine and does not do them will be like a foolish man who built his house on the sand. And the rain fell, and the floods came, and the winds blew and beat against that house, and it fell, and great was the fall of it."*
>
> MATTHEW 7:24-27

In sum, Jesus calls us to live a life that is centered on God, lived in reliance on his power and his goodness. Our lives are centered on God if we do everything for his glory, not our own. Our lives are lived in reliance on his power and his goodness if we acknowledge that without him we can do nothing.

Once we understand this truth—that faithful obedience to God is the only way to lasting contentment and joy—then we are ready for the next: God wants our complete obedience. If we wish to be free of sin in our daily life, we must submit ourselves as slaves to Christ (Romans 6:17-22).

Put differently, obedience requires more than half measures. When Christ calls us to follow him, he demands to be our top priority:

> *As they were going along the road, someone said to him, "I will follow you wherever you go." And Jesus said to him, "Foxes have holes, and birds of the air have nests, but the Son of Man has nowhere to lay his head." To another he said, "Follow me." But he said, "Lord, let me first go and bury my father." And Jesus said to him, "Leave the dead to bury their own dead. But as for you, go and proclaim the kingdom of God." Yet another said, "I will follow you, Lord, but let me first say farewell to those at my home." Jesus said to him, "No one who puts his hand to the plow and looks back is fit for the kingdom of God."*
>
> LUKE 9:57-62

If this feels overwhelming, we should take heart. Christ's yoke is easy and his burden is light (Matthew 11:28-30). He is a gentle master, and his commandments are not burdensome. We were made to live lives of humble obedience to God. To the extent

---

[10] Matthew 5-7.

we do, we experience the fullness of what it means to be human. Our experience shows this to be true.

In demanding our obedience Christ is inviting us into his rest. In Christ, we can cast off our anxieties and find the peace of God.[11] When we begin to do things God's way, we are no longer working against the grain of his creation, and we will discover the secret to contentment in all circumstances (Philippians 4:11-13).

So, while we think that it is no small thing to entrust ourselves to Christ, it is also what we are made to do. Our spiritual rebirth may be a once-for-all event, but continuing to entrust ourselves to Christ is a lifetime process. We must die to ourselves and live to Christ every day (1 Corinthians 15:31).

STEP THREE PRACTICAL APPLICATION

If you are prepared to take (or retake) this step and offer yourself to God to do with as he pleases, we have a few practical suggestions.

Verbal Prayer. Provided you are willing to continue with this process, we suggest that you verbally entrust yourself to God—his care and provision—in the form of prayer. We don't want to prescribe a formulaic prayer, but as a helpful starting point, your prayer might sound something like this:

> Father, I entrust myself to your grace through faith in your son, Jesus Christ, the great prophet, priest, and king. Create in me a submissive heart and a willing spirit, to do your will obediently in all aspects of my life. Do with me as you wish, and transform me into who you want me to be. Relieve me from the bondage of sin, so that I might better do your will, and that victory over sin may bear witness to your power and your glory. I pray these things on the authority of your son, Jesus Christ.

Formal Commitment. We also suggest that you treat this step as a formal commitment to God, yourself, and your sponsor to continue through the rest of the steps outlined in this book, and to diligently seek to submit to God in all aspects of your life.

View it as an experiment of sorts: a commitment to do things God's way for a season, to gain a deeper understanding of what Jesus meant when he said, "If you keep my commandments, you will abide in my love, just as I have kept my Father's commandments and abide in his love. These things I have spoken to you, that my joy may be in you, and that your joy may be full" (John 15:10-11).

Experience has shown us that when we do things God's way, joy results, just as Jesus promised—and we are confident that your experience will show you the same thing,

---

[11] *Cf.* Matthew 11:28-30; Exodus 33:14; Hebrews 4:1-11.

if you seek to obey him.

Get started! The way you know you've done a good third step is if you immediately continue to the fourth step. If you find yourself tempted to dawdle or delay, ask yourself whether you have any lingering reservations and doubts. If so, share these with others and try to work through them.

STEP FOUR
SELF-EXAMINATION

"For no good tree bears bad fruit, nor again does a bad tree bear good fruit, for each tree is known by its own fruit. For figs are not gathered from thornbushes, nor are grapes picked from a bramble bush. The good person out of the good treasure of his heart produces good, and the evil person out of his evil treasure produces evil, for out of the abundance of the heart his mouth speaks."

LUKE 6:43-45

Our particular sins are not the cause of the problem; they are the manifestation of the problem. Sins are only symptoms, whereas sinfulness (*i.e.,* being a "sinner") is the disease. We are not sinful because we sin; we sin because we are sinful (or at least our flesh is). Bad trees bear bad fruit. They cannot bear good fruit (Luke 6:43-44).

Here it may help to clarify terms.

What is a sin? A "sin" is any thought or action (or inaction) that does not correspond to God's revealed will. It is tempting to reduce God's will to a set of dos and don'ts, but it is more than that. Obeying God's will requires that we:

- **Do the right thing:** obey God's law (1 John 3:4).

- **Do it for the right goal:** glorify God (1 Corinthians 10:31).

- **Do it with right motivations:** in faith and love (Romans 14:23, 1 Corinthians 13:1-3).[12]

If we do the right thing towards the right goal and with the right motivations, we are acting righteously. If we act in any other way, we sin. Thus, obviously, we sin when we do the wrong thing (disobey God). But we also sin when we do the right thing with wrong motives (*e.g.,* give offerings to increase our stature in the community). And we even sin when we do the right thing for the right reason but for the wrong end (*e.g.,* give offerings out of love but without regard for whether God is glorified). This understanding of sin should help us see that we all sin far more than we realize.

What is it to be sinful? To be "sinful" is to be in our natural, unredeemed state, apart from Christ. Though as with most words, "sinful" can carry a range of meanings— the most frequent meaning in the New Testament is to describe someone who is not

---

[12] *See* John M. Frame, *Systematic Theology: An Introduction to Christian Belief* (Phillipsburg: P&R Publishing Company, 2013), 848–51.

in right relationship with God. It primarily denotes the state of human beings before they are saved by grace and thereby cleansed, justified, and given new hearts.

It is easy to confuse sin and its cause, and then try to treat the symptoms rather than the disease. This, we think, is a mistake. If we are seriously ill, suppressing the symptoms may make us more comfortable, but it will complicate our diagnosis and treatment. The same is true for our sins. If a man musters all his strength to suppress his rage when people do not do as he wishes, he is liable to believe that he is not a controlling person. If he goes to great length to avoid the opposite sex, he may trick himself into believing he is not lustful. In each case, though, he is only addressing the symptoms, while ignoring the fact that he is suffering from a terminal disease.

This means that any successful attempt to address our sin must start by addressing our sinfulness. It will do us no good to mask our symptoms if the disease continues to ravage us. Rather, we must first cast ourselves upon Christ, the Great Physician. He alone can restore us to right relationship with God through his perfect sacrifice and merciful intercessions and heal our diseased heart. Otherwise, we are only treating our symptoms, which may make us feel better, but will leave the real problem unaddressed. It is only through the gift of spiritual life that we are able to be free of sin.

As believers, we have made a good beginning. We have been reborn and have a new spiritual nature, united with Christ and empowered by the Holy Spirit.

But the story does not end here. We now have a spiritual nature, but we still have our natural, sinful nature as well, and this old nature still exerts considerable influence over us.[13]

The Apostle Paul uses two primary images to illustrate this process. The first illustration is the imagery of an old self and a new self. We have an "old self" who belongs to our former manner of life and is still corrupted by deceitful desires, and we have a "new self," who has been created after the likeness of God in righteousness and holiness (Ephesians 4:22-24). We are called to "put off" our old self and "put on" our new self. The second illustration is the imagery of our flesh and our spirit. We have "flesh," which is hostile to God, incapable of submitting to his law, and unable to please God (Romans 8:6-8). We also have a renewed "spirit," given to us by the Holy Spirit in our conversion, whereby we have new life and righteousness (Romans 8:9-11). The Christian walk is one of putting to death the deeds of the flesh, on the one hand, and walking according to the Spirit, on the other.[14]

---

[13] *Cf.* Romans 7:21-25.
[14] *Cf.* Romans 8:13; Galatians 5:16-25; Colossians 3:1-17.

Both images point to the same reality: though we are no longer "sinful," we are still full of sin, and we are called to spend the rest of our lives rooting it out by means of God's grace.[15]

This truth sets the tone of our personal inventory. The point of personal inventory is self-examination, not just tallying up our sins. Sinfulness has a way of masquerading as self-righteousness, and our deceitful hearts have a way of justifying and rationalizing our sins. Personal inventory is a tool to allow us to see through these lies and diagnose what sinful passions still lurk in our heart, so that we can confess them to God and let his grace flow in and transform us. Experience shows us that we can see these passions most clearly in our resentments, fears, and sexuality, so we focus on these, but every person's passions show themselves somewhat differently.

As we prepare to begin the inventory process, we should keep in mind three truths:

First, we are incapable of seeing the extent of our own sin without God's help. In our natural state, our minds and hearts are darkened by self-delusion (Romans 1:21). We need God to shine his light into our hearts before we can see the darkness clearly. So, we should always begin by asking God for help.

Second, we cannot change our hearts any more than the leopard can change his spots (Jeremiah 13:23). Only Christ can do that. So, our sanctification must start and end with faith in him. Yet we have a part to play in our sanctification[16], and here our job is to take a careful look at our heart and begin to honestly assess our problems. As with anything else, we cannot do this without God's help, and so we should prepare ourselves through prayer, asking him to give us spiritual transformation.

Third, as Christians who have been united with Christ, we are free from sin's penalty (Romans 5:1, 8:1). We can still sin, of course, but there is no penalty for sin under the New Covenant because Christ has already paid all our debts in full.[17] We have as our High Priest the perfect Son of God who constantly makes intercessions with the Father on our behalf and gives us confidence to draw near to God (Hebrews 4:14-16). We must firmly grasp this truth if we are to face our sin honestly without falling into despair. We can look at our sin without shrinking back because we know that it has already been paid for, and we can pray for assurance of pardon.

The remainder of this chapter will explain some of the inventory tools we have found to be simple yet effective for helping with this process. **Appendix B** will include

---

[15] In theological terms, this process is called sanctification. Literally, "sanctification" means the process of becoming more holy or sanctified (being set apart). In one sense, we are sanctified when we become believers (hence we are called "saints"). But in another sense, we experience ongoing sanctification throughout the rest of our lives. The Bible uses the term in both ways, but the meaning can typically be determined by context.

[16] *Cf.* Philippians 2:12-13.

[17] *Cf.* Jeremiah 31:34.

several types of inventories that may be helpful for your particular situation.

Before we begin, we have a few preliminary notes based on our experience. First, we have found that a written inventory is the most effective. Writing the inventory down helps focus our thoughts and allows us to see more clearly the patterns to our struggle. Second, we have found it best to begin the inventory process as soon as possible after resolving to take one, preferably immediately after. Procrastination is the enemy of effective recovery. Third, we have found that it is best not to wait too long to finish the inventory. No matter how busy we are, we have found that someone who genuinely wants to recover can complete a thorough inventory in two weeks or less, and certainly within one month. Lastly, we have found that it is best to follow instructions precisely, at least for our first inventory, in order to best learn the process.

For those recovering from addiction and compulsive behaviors, we recommend four basic inventories: a "resentment inventory," a "fear inventory," a "sex inventory," and a "shame/guilt inventory."

A resentment inventory is a catalogue of the things that make us upset, angry, or resentful. A fear inventory is a catalogue of the things that cause us fear and anxiety. A sexual inventory is a catalogue of our past relationships and sexual misconduct. A guilt and shame inventory is a catalogue of our sources of guilt and shame. Example inventories are provided in **Appendix B**.

For each inventory, we ask four basic questions: (1) who/what, (2) how was I affected, (3) what was my part, and (4) how am I doubting God?

For the first question, we are asking about the nature of the resentment, fear, or sexual issue. It can be a person, an institution, a principle, or anything else. It can be big or small, recent or in the distant past. It should be a short reminder ("He fired me"), not an in-depth analysis of the problem. If it comes to mind, we should put it down. These are diagnostic tools, after all, so the more data the better.

For the second question, we find it helpful to focus on four basic desires:

- **Power.** "How does this affect my desire for power over other people?"

- **Approval.** "How does this affect my desire for approval or affirmation (including respect)?"

- **Comfort.** "How does this affect my desire for comfort or pleasure?"

- **Security.** "How does this affect my desire for security and control over circumstances?"[18]

For the third question, we find it helpful to focus on four basic ways we fall short of God's law: selfishness, dishonesty, self-seeking, and fear. In other words, we ask four questions:

- **Selfish.** "How did I fail to consider others?"

- **Dishonest.** "What was I unwilling to admit?"

- **Self-Seeking.** "How was I trying to glorify myself?"

- **Afraid.** "What was I afraid to lose?

For the fourth column, we also examine how we are failing to believe God's truth. In other words, we ask ourselves what aspect of God's truth, if believed more fully, would help address this issue.

In filling out this last column, it is important to note that God promises to take care of us, but he does not promise to give us everything we think we want (or even everything we think we need). Instead, he promises to make us holy and lavish us with spiritual blessings, which is what we really want and what we really need. Sometimes this entails a season of material abundance and comfort, but sometimes this entails a season of loss and suffering. In either event, God is providentially at work to bring about his will: our sanctification.

If we have done this step correctly, we have made a good beginning. We will have begun to comprehend the effect our sin has had in our lives, as well as areas of weakness where we are particularly prone to sin. But this is not a stopping place. All we have done is a diagnostic. We understand the problem, but we have not yet laid hold of a solution. We must work the rest of the steps to find a solution.

STEP FOUR PRACTICAL APPLICATION

Pray for willingness, honesty, and clarity. If you find yourself unwilling to look at yourself honestly, don't worry—you're not alone. We are all incapable of honestly examining and assessing our faults. We must have God's help. We can search our hearts only because God searches our hearts with us (Psalm 139:23-24). So, before we begin, we should petition God for willingness, honesty, and most of all, clarity.

Prepare your inventories. We suggest you complete the inventories outlined in this chapter (resentment, fear, sex, and shame). Procrastination is the main enemy here. If you think more inventories would be helpful, we encourage you to do those as well.

---

[18] *See* Timothy Keller, *Counterfeit Gods: The Empty Promises of Money, Sex, and Power, and the Only Hope that Matters* (New York: Penguin Group, 2009).

But the trick is simply to get started—these are never as hard as they seem. Three practical tips:

- **Make time.** Set aside at least one hour a day to work on your inventory.

- **Do your inventories one at a time.** Finish with your resentment inventory before you move onto fear, then sex.

- **Finish one column at a time.** Finish with column 1 (who/what and why) before moving onto column 2 (heart idolatry), and so forth.

Breaking it down this way makes it easier to get started and makes it easier to see patterns emerge.

God-centered relationships. When cataloging significant relationships, we find it helpful to also ask ourselves, "How would this relationship have been different if I had put God at the center?" Answering this question allows us to not only examine what we did wrong, but what we could have done right instead. In this way, we begin to form an idea of what healthy, godly relationships look like—whether romantic or platonic.

STEP FIVE
CONFESSION

Whoever conceals his transgressions will not prosper, but he who confesses and forsakes them will obtain mercy.

PROVERBS 28:13

It may seem strange that confession of sin plays such an outsized role in Christian practice, given that it is only explicitly commanded twice in the entire New Testament.[19] This fact, coupled with a correct conviction that we have been completely forgiven by virtue of Christ's finished work, has understandably led many to erroneously reject the idea that we have any need to confess our sins at all, let alone confess them to other people (at least outside of the context of direct reconciliation with the offended party). We are certainly not in a position to ignore any commands in scripture, no matter how prominent. Additionally, our experience is that confession of sin, both to God and to other people, has a valuable role in the recovery process.

The New Testament suggests confession to God and to others is appropriate in three contexts.

First, confession of sin is an appropriate companion to turning to God in faith. There is a clear biblical basis for asserting that when we turn to God, we can and should follow that turning with confessing our sins, particularly upon first coming to faith.[20] In acknowledging our savior, it is appropriate to acknowledge that we need saving. In other words, as we turn away from self and turn towards God, it is appropriate to acknowledge both to God and to others the nature of our error. Confession is emphatically not a prerequisite to justification, but it is a suitable complement to it.

Second, confession of sin is an appropriate means to cleanse ourselves of feelings of guilt. As King David acknowledged and his son Solomon confirmed, when we bottle up our sins, they drain us of spiritual vitality (Psalm 32:3-5; Proverbs 28:13). Thus, confessing our sins to God is a means by which we apply God's gracious forgiveness in our day-to-day life in a way that purifies us and frees us from feelings of guilt and defilement that results from sin (1 John 1:9).

Third, confession of sins within the context of Christian community, together with prayer, is an appropriate way to effect healing (James 5:16). Though the Bible

---

[19] James 5:16 and 1 John 1:9.
[20] *Cf.* Matthew 3:6; Mark 1:5; Acts 19:18.

is not clear on why precisely this is true, our experience suggests that being open about our struggle with sin opens the door for them helping us with wise counsel and instruction (Proverbs 11:14, 15:22, 20:18). God has placed us in Christian community to restore each other with gentleness and help each other carry burdens (Galatians 6:1-2, 5). The successful operation of this principle relies, in no small part, on honesty about our struggles.

We find it helpful to structure this step to account for all three of these uses. First, because confession is a companion to turning to God, we should honestly describe the person we were but no longer wish to be, thereby rooting out the "old self" and exposing him to the light of Christ. Second, because confession frees us from the burden of our guilt, we should be diligent in confessing all our sins to God and to another person so that we can feel sin's power of guilt and shame fall away and begin to see more clearly the forgiveness we have in Christ. Third, because confession allows us to seek counsel and advice from another person, we should be willing to hear their perspective and grateful for their insight.. Others can often see things we cannot, and by disclosing our problem to someone else we allow them to speak truth to us in love.

Therefore, we recommend that you sit down with a spiritual advisor (such as a sponsor, mentor, or pastor) both to review the inventories you have prepared and to confess any sins that may be weighing on your conscience. The aim is to look for patterns and areas of weakness and help set you free from guilt and shame. What counts most here is thoroughness and honesty. Just as it is difficult to correctly diagnose a disease unless you list all your symptoms, it will be difficult to correctly diagnose your sinful tendencies unless you are completely honest about how they manifest.

In taking this step, we suggest that you neither dawdle nor rush. Lay out the facts simply, honestly, and completely. The goal is to be thorough and get to the heart of the issue.

A note of caution: it is sometimes easy to lapse into boasting or self-flagellation. Some of us treated our past sins as badges of honor showing how tough, crafty, or powerful we were. We tried to one-up each other to prove that we were indeed the "first among sinners." Others used this process to show how awful and shameful we were. We insisted on continuing to shame ourselves for sins that Christ had already removed. Both behaviors are exercises in pride: the pride that says we are worse than others or that we have any sin too great for Christ's forgiveness. In either case, we lack a proper perspective, and we should remind ourselves that this process is about facing facts and feeling forgiveness, not self-glorification or self-flagellation.

More than anything else, however, this process of self-examination and confession should reveal the precise extent of our problem. The central fact we are called to face is that we are completely dependent upon Christ's righteousness to justify us and his Holy Spirit to sanctify us. This process should have revealed specific areas of weakness, but more than that, it should have revealed that we ourselves are weak. We could resolve to change all we wanted, but what we typically found was that we'd resolve to change one day and be back at it the next. When we examined our lives, we found that our self-salvation project was a failure. Christ is the only sure foundation for change (1 Corinthians 3:10-15). In this way, a close look at our legal track record should reveal our need for Christ, not our plan for self-directed change.

In closing, we must stress that confession is not a mechanical process. It is easy to slip into legalism and offer up mechanical prayers to God in an effort to remove uncomfortable feelings of guilt but without any real desire to change.[21] If we do this, we risk reducing Christ to a system of rules, rather than a good and just ruler, brother, lord, servant, and, of course, God. To guard against this error, we must constantly remind ourselves that confession, by itself, affords no grace. Grace comes from God alone, and that through faith in Christ.

STEP FIVE PRACTICAL APPLICATION

In terms of practically putting this step into action, we recommend a simple three-part process:

Pray for willingness. Just as we were not entirely willing to examine ourselves in the fourth step, we will not be entirely willing to be open about ourselves in the fifth step. The temptation will be to hide and deflect. So, at the outset, we recommend asking God for honesty and willingness in this process.

Share your inventory with another. As we mentioned above, the simplest way to put this step into action is to sit down with a sponsor, spiritual advisor, pastor, or even trusted friend and share your inventory with him or her. Solicit input during this process—he or she will often be able to see things about yourself that you cannot. The goal is to get a better understanding of yourself, your heart idols, your habitual sins, and the makeup of your soul.

Confess anything else not on your inventory. The biblical commands to confess your sins are not limited to the types of sins that would show up on the inventories we have suggested. If we have other sins that are not listed on one of our inventories, we should confess them to God and to our sponsor as we share our inventory. When we

---

[21] *Cf.* 2 Corinthians 7:9-11.

are finished, we want to have shared everything with another person.

Receive feedback. When you are finished sharing, ask your sponsor what heart idols he or she identified in the process. The goal here is not to have your sponsor beat up on you—it's for you and your sponsor together to work to identify the sin lurking in your heart so that you can work together to uproot it.

STEP SIX
COMMITMENT

We know that Christ, being raised from the dead, will never die again; death no longer has dominion over him. For the death he died he died to sin, once for all, but the life he lives he lives to God. So you also must consider yourselves dead to sin and alive to God in Christ Jesus.

Let not sin therefore reign in your mortal body, to make you obey its passions. Do not present your members to sin as instruments for unrighteousness, but present yourselves to God as those who have been brought from death to life, and your members to God as instruments for righteousness. For sin will have no dominion over you, since you are not under law but under grace.

What then? Are we to sin because we are not under law but under grace? By no means! Do you not know that if you present yourselves to anyone as obedient slaves, you are slaves of the one whom you obey, either of sin, which leads to death, or of obedience, which leads to righteousness? But thanks be to God, that you who were once slaves of sin have become obedient from the heart to the standard of teaching to which you were committed, and, having been set free from sin, have become slaves of righteousness. I am speaking in human terms, because of your natural limitations. For just as you once presented your members as slaves to impurity and to lawlessness leading to more lawlessness, so now present your members as slaves to righteousness leading to sanctification.

ROMANS 6:9-19

It is a spiritual axiom that no one can serve two masters. If you love one, then you will hate the other; if you are devoted to one, then you will despise the other (Matthew 6:24).

In his Letter to the Romans, the Apostle Paul explains how this truth applies to our Christian walk. As Christians, we live between masters. On the one hand, having been justified by Christ's blood, we are now free from the mastery of sin. We have died with Christ to sin, so that we might no longer be slaves to sin, and have been raised with him too, in order that we might walk in newness of life (Romans 6:4-8). On the other hand, sin is still very much at work in us, even as believers, and will continue to be at work in us until we are finally delivered from our mortal bodies by Christ (Romans 7:13-25). The rest of our lives will be characterized by a battle between two competing natures: our sinful flesh and our renewed spirit.

So now we have a choice. If it is a spiritual axiom that we cannot serve two masters, it is also a spiritual axiom that the one we serve is, in effect, our master. If we listen to and obey sin, then sin will be our master. If we listen to and obey God, then God will be our master (Romans 6:16).

It is in this context that the Apostle Paul gives us two very specific commands.

First, we must consider ourselves dead to sin and alive to God in Christ Jesus (Romans 6:11). This command is not an exercise in spiritual make-believe; it is a reminder of the power that is now at work within us. Sin has no claim on us and it cannot demand that we follow its commands (Romans 6:14). As believers, we will never be presented with a temptation that we are not able to resist, in reliance on God's power, provided we choose to do so.[22]

Second, we must not let sin reign over us to make us obey its passions (Romans 6:12). This command has both a negative and a positive aspect.

Negatively, we are instructed not to present our members to sin as instruments for unrighteousness (Romans 6:13a). In other words, we are told to refrain from sinning. When we sin, we nourish our sinful natures, making them stronger and more demanding. We will not see any victory in our battle with sin unless we are ready and willing to fight rather than surrender.

Positively, we are instructed to present ourselves to God as those who have been brought from death to life, and then to present our members to God as instruments for righteousness (Romans 6:13b, 19). Growing in holiness requires more than attempting to refrain from sin (though it does not require less than that!). Self-denial alone will fail because it fails to understand the problem. We sin because our hearts long for the wrong things. Our God-given instincts have been perverted and distorted into idolatrous longings. We cannot suppress these instincts any more than we can suppress our instincts for food and water. Instead, we must let God reorient these instincts so that they find their greatest fulfillment in God and his gifts.[23] Christ offers us rest for our wearied and heavy-laden souls, but we must first take up his yoke and let him teach us about true happiness (Matthew 11:28-30).

A practical illustration may be helpful here. Imagine a man has a job that is miserable and unfulfilling. His employer was cruel and dishonest, with no regard for his employee's well-being. Now imagine that man is offered a new job that is both enjoyable and fulfilling, with an excellent employer. Naturally, he takes the new job. But his old employer keeps calling, ordering him to show up to work. He doesn't need to obey his old employer, so he doesn't. Instead, he shows up at his new employment. Next, his old employer tries to entice him with promises of rewards. Again our man

---

[22] *Cf.* 1 Corinthians 10:13; Hebrews 2:18; James 4:7.
[23] *Cf.* Jeremiah 2:13; John 4:13-14; Romans 6:22-23.

declines, knowing that his old employer's promises are worthless and that he has a new employer whom he enjoys working for anyway. Lastly, the old employer tries to get our man to do work for him on the side while he's at his new place of employment. Our man declines this as well, devoting himself instead to working for his current employer. The Apostle Paul's instructions can be summarized in these three points: when you get a new job, (1) stop showing up to your old job, (2) start showing up to your new job, and (3) don't do any work on the side.

This illustration tracks on another level, too. Being a good employee entails more than simply showing up to work and doing what your employer asks you to. Being a good employee means showing up eager and ready to work ("present yourselves to God"), and then putting your talents to good use in the workplace ("[present] your members to God as instruments for righteousness"). Effectively serving God requires more than keeping the rules and rote performance of duty. It requires serving God, as a person. It means presenting ourselves to him as a living sacrifice to be renewed by his grace and transformed into instruments to serve his purposes.[24]

As a corollary to these principles, we should add another: if we want to be free from sin, we must want to be free from sin completely. We must aim for universal obedience in all areas of our lives if we expect to see victory in our specific struggle. If we wish to be free of a particular sin without wishing to be obedient in the other areas of our life, it is not our sinfulness that we hate, but the consequences of a particular sin. It is good to hate particular sins and their consequences, but we are called to hate our sinfulness, and all the sins it produces, irrespective of the consequences. If we wish to experience God's blessings, we ought not to be particular in our duties.[25] Our obedience is a crucial means by which we break the power of sin in our lives. If we are not obedient, we have no right to expect the power of sin to be broken, any more than someone who does not exercise should expect to grow stronger. In fact, in many cases we felt as if God allowed us to fail in particular ways to reveal how we have failed in more general ways, and thereby draw us closer to him.[26] Therefore, we must heed the Apostle Paul's command to cleanse ourselves of all pollution and perfect our holiness in the fear of God (2 Corinthians 7:1).

STEP SIX PRACTICAL APPLICATION

Willingness. We must ask ourselves if we are willing to completely present ourselves to God in this way on a daily basis. Knowing that his yoke is easy and his burden is light, are we willing to submit to be Christ's servants?

---

[24] *Cf.* Romans 12:1-8; Ephesians 4:22-24.
[25] *Cf.* Isaiah 58:2-7; Matthew 23:23; Luke 11:42.
[26] Compare John 18:25-27 with 21:15-19.

Dependency. No one is ever truly ready to surrender themselves completely to God, and so we must recognize that we need God's help even in asking him for help. The next chapter addresses what it looks like to surrender ourselves to God, and what God does to transform our hearts.

STEP SEVEN
GRACE

But by the grace of God I am what I am, and his grace toward me was not in vain. On the contrary, I worked harder than any of them, though it was not I, but the grace of God that is with me.

1 CORINTHIANS 15:10

Therefore, my beloved, as you have always obeyed, so now, not only as in my presence but much more in my absence, work out your own salvation with fear and trembling, for it is God who works in you, both to will and to work for his good pleasure.

PHILIPPIANS 2:12-13

Now may the God of peace himself sanctify you completely, and may your whole spirit and soul and body be kept blameless at the coming of our Lord Jesus Christ. He who calls you is faithful; he will surely do it.

1 THESSALONIANS 5:23-24

If the Bible clearly affirms that we have a part to play in our sanctification, it also clearly affirms that God does as well (often in the same sentence).

But what part precisely does God play? It is easy enough to affirm that God's grace creates the conditions for growth—He made us alive in Christ and now we are set free to serve him! But the Bible goes further than that. God does not simply allow or enable us to grow spiritually; he actually does it for us.[27] His grace is within us, performing our work for us. He not only wills our sanctification, he actually works it out.

This truth should inform our pursuit of holiness. It does not, of course, nullify our personal responsibility to diligently pursue holiness—something the Bible explicitly commands in several places. But it does help put our pursuit of holiness in perspective. We will grow in our personal holiness to the extent that we cooperate with God working on and in us.

It is fairly simple to understand how God works *on* us. As the author of Hebrews notes, our good heavenly father trains and disciplines us just as a good human father trains and disciplines his children:

---

[27] *Cf.* 1 Corinthians 15:10; Philippians 2:13; 1 Thessalonians 5:24.

> *It is for discipline that you have to endure. God is treating you as sons. For what son is there whom his father does not discipline? If you are left without discipline, in which all have participated, then you are illegitimate children and not sons. Besides this, we have had earthly fathers who disciplined us and we respected them. Shall we not much more be subject to the Father of spirits and live? For they disciplined us for a short time as it seemed best to them, but he disciplines us for our good, that we may share his holiness. For the moment, all discipline seems painful rather than pleasant, but later it yields the peaceful fruit of righteousness to those who have been trained by it.*
>
> HEBREWS 12:7-11

God disciplines us because we are his adopted children. Importantly, unlike a human parent whose discipline can sometimes be arbitrary or capricious, subject to moods and mistakes, God's discipline is perfect and for our good. True, it can be painful at the time, but it always yields the fruit of righteousness. For him, it is a labor of love (Hebrews 12:6).

It is more complex to understand how God works *in* us. In fact, this process itself is complex, because God is working in us in a variety of ways. First, God awakens and empowers us with his grace (1 Corinthians 15:10). Second, God provides us with what we need to do his will (Hebrews 13:21a). Third, God makes us desire to do his will, what is good (Hebrews 13:21b). Fourth, God spurs on our actual choices so that this desire results in action (Philippians 2:13). In short, he has sealed us with his Spirit who dwells in us, who continues to turn our hearts to God and who guarantees our inheritance until we actually acquire possession of it. We are "strengthened with power through his Spirit" in our inner being, so that "Christ may dwell in [our] hearts through faith," and thereby we might be "filled with all the fullness of God" (Ephesians 3:15-19).

None of this, of course, is to discount our own responsibility. We have received the Spirit, and now we must live and walk by it and refrain from gratifying our sinful desires. God is working in and for us, and therefore we are instructed to work as well. The grace of God is at work in us and therefore we must work as hard as we can to live godly lives. Knowing that God is at work in us is not an excuse to relax or take it easy; it is a reason to work harder than ever, knowing that we can do, endure, suffer, and overcome anything through Christ who strengthens us.[28]

But our work should be done in the proper way. There is a sort of "spiritual" effort that lacks any transformative power. It is the easiest and most natural thing in the world to develop and rely upon rituals and routines to make us holy rather than relying upon the Holy Spirit to guide us through faith. Spiritual transformation comes from the triune God through faith—God the Father ordains our sanctification, God the

---

[28] *Cf.* Galatians 5:16-25; 1 Corinthians 15:10; Philippians 4:13.

Son secures it, and God the Spirit applies it to our lives—not by checking boxes or doing duties, even good and proper duties. Christianity is not a system to be worked; it is a relationship to be built.

This statement should not be taken to suggest that a methodical or disciplined approach to spiritual growth is wrong, of course. External obedience and spiritual routine are necessary to grow, in the same way that fidelity and responsibility are necessary to a healthy marriage. But they are not sufficient. And they are no substitute for a relationship with God in Christ.

Therefore, any lasting spiritual change must begin and end with God, the author of our salvation. If we want to grow and change, we must ask God to grow us and change us.

More importantly, any lasting spiritual change must begin and end with God's will, not our own. God is far more concerned with our personal holiness than we are. In fact, God has had a plan for every believer's sanctification that has been in place since before the foundation of the world (Ephesians 1:4). He is far more knowledgeable than us about how to restore us to the image of his son and make us into who we were meant to be. He is the master builder, and the church is his masterpiece, a holy temple for his Holy Spirit (Ephesians 2:19-22). It simply will not do to tell him how to carve the stones, where they should fit, or how we think the building should be proportioned. Put differently, the clay does not tell the potter what to do.[29] We must trust him, let him do his work, and submit to him in it, praying that his will, not ours, be done.

If we are ready to submit to God's work on and in us, we should petition him in prayer immediately—and repeatedly, every day, so long as it is called today—to change us according to his will, to make us into who he wants us to be, and for the willingness to submit to that process in faith. And then we must be ready to respond with more action.

STEP SEVEN PRACTICAL APPLICATION

Verbal prayer. As with step three, we suggest that you meet with your sponsor and, in the form of a prayer, verbally ask God for his transformative grace. We don't want to prescribe a formulaic prayer, but as a helpful starting point, your prayer might sound something like this:

> Father, help me submit to your transforming grace, and help me grow into the likeness of Christ. Train me to renounce ungodliness and worldly passions; help me

---

[29] *Cf.* Romans 9:21.

to live a self-controlled, upright, and godly life; and fill me with hope for the return of our great God and Savior Jesus Christ. Grant that I might shine forth your light into the darkness and be salt to a perishing world. I pray these things for your glory and on the authority of your Son, Jesus Christ.

We should not pray this sort of prayer once and check it off our list. Rather, we continue to ask God in this way to change us every day, working daily towards a great dependence on his grace.

Formal commitment. As with step three, we also suggest that you treat this step as a formal commitment to God, yourself, and your sponsor to continue on through the rest of the steps outlined in this book, and to diligently seek to submit to God in all aspects of your life, trusting that he will graciously provide for us in that process.

Get started! The way you know you've done a good seventh step is if you immediately continue on to the eighth step. If you find yourself tempted to delay, ask yourself whether you have any lingering reservations and doubts. If so, share these to others and try to work through them.

STEP EIGHT
FORGIVENESS

Then Peter came up and said to him, "Lord, how often will my brother sin against me, and I forgive him? As many as seven times?" Jesus said to him, "I do not say to you seven times, but seventy-seven times.

"Therefore the kingdom of heaven may be compared to a king who wished to settle accounts with his servants. When he began to settle, one was brought to him who owed him ten thousand talents. And since he could not pay, his master ordered him to be sold, with his wife and children and all that he had, and payment to be made. So the servant fell on his knees, imploring him, 'Have patience with me, and I will pay you everything.' And out of pity for him, the master of that servant released him and forgave him the debt. But when that same servant went out, he found one of his fellow servants who owed him a hundred denarii, and seizing him, he began to choke him, saying, 'Pay what you owe.' So his fellow servant fell down and pleaded with him, 'Have patience with me, and I will pay you.' He refused and went and put him in prison until he should pay the debt. When his fellow servants saw what had taken place, they were greatly distressed, and they went and reported to their master all that had taken place. Then his master summoned him and said to him, 'You wicked servant! I forgave you all that debt because you pleaded with me. And should not you have had mercy on your fellow servant, as I had mercy on you?' And in anger his master delivered him to the jailers, until he should pay all his debt. So also my heavenly Father will do to every one of you, if you do not forgive your brother from your heart."

MATTHEW 18:21-35

Most of us struggle with seeking forgiveness from others because we focus on the wrongs (real or perceived) that those same people have done to us. Ironically, the largest barrier to our seeking forgiveness from others is usually our own unforgiving heart.[30] When we have committed an unreciprocated wrong, it is easy enough to make amends, provided we can push through the awkwardness of doing so. But this situation is quite rare indeed. Far more often, there is sin on both sides of the ledger. We find ourselves asked to humble ourselves and ask forgiveness from someone who has wronged us, sometimes quite severely. And our prideful hearts tend to balk at this indignity. Rarely is the person we have wronged entirely innocent in the matter—and even when they are innocent, our slanderous hearts can fabricate a perceived wrong to rationalize our behavior.

So, before we can begin the process of seeking forgiveness, we must first forgive those who have wronged us. Thus, if we are to be effective in this step, we must tame our

---

[30] *See* Matthew 7:2.

unforgiving hearts. We can do this in two main ways. First, we can petition God for help. Knowing that we are not willing to make amends, we can ask God to make us willing. Second, we can rehearse God's truths to remind ourselves of how we ought to act and why.

The first of these truths is that the Lord is judge, and we are not. When we pass judgment on others for their wrongs, we play God (James 4:12). Doing so is emphatically not our place. It is a challenge of God's holy authority. When we pass judgment on others, we are like a presumptuous child playing the role of scolding parent to her misbehaving brother. To her, it may seem like she is doing a good thing for her parents in making sure her brother follows their rules. But from the outside looking in, it is obvious that this child is getting too big for her britches. She fancies herself as her parents' equal instead of a fellow child under their authority. It is an exercise in conceit.

The second of these truths is that we must be conduits of God's mercy. We are all sinners saved by grace. Because God forgave us, we are called to forgive others, even (or perhaps especially) when they do not deserve forgiveness. In a fit of anger, we may demand that justice be done, but the truth is that if justice were done, we ourselves would be condemned. When we demand justice, we are like the unforgiving servant. God has forgiven us an incalculable debt. We are now in no position to turn around and demand repayment of a few pennies from our own debtors.[31] We were not put here on this earth to settle scores with people who have harmed us. We were put here to be God's representatives and to live for his glory.

STEP EIGHT PRACTICAL APPLICATION

Ask God for help. We ask God to give us the willingness to make our amends, and the insight to get to the heart of the issue. If we feel judgmental or angry, we ask for help about that, as well. We ask God to help us see when we are being unworthy servants—demanding payment of small debts from others, even though we've been forgiven large debts by God. In short, we recognize that we cannot make amends to others properly without God's aid.

Pray for our enemies. A simple yet effective way to overcome a bitter, unforgiving attitude towards others is to pray for those people (Matthew 5:44). In doing so, we begin the process of un-hardening our hearts. It is difficult to harbor resentment towards someone, while at the same time earnestly petitioning God for them. A good method is to pray for them for two weeks, asking God to draw them closer to himself and to grant us a forgiving, understanding, and compassionate heart towards

---

[31] *Cf.* Matthew 18:23-35.

them. By the end, we will discover that God has answered our prayers.

Prepare and discuss your amends with your sponsor. Having asked God for his aid and being armed with these truths, it is now time to get practical. Our experience is that few people are experts in frankly making amends with those they have harmed. Sometimes our amends are little more than empty apologies. Sometimes they are obvious attempts at manipulation. Sometimes they are exercises in blame-shifting and excuse-making. In almost every case, they are inadequate in some way. Therefore, most of us have found it helpful to think through (and perhaps even sketch out in writing) how we plan to make amends and then discuss the matter carefully with our sponsor. While we do not wish to prescribe an exact formula, some preparatory work with your sponsor will help guard against carelessness and also give us confidence about what we will say.

Seek wise counsel on difficult amends. Many of us have done things that, if admitted, would bring consequences for us and for others. We recognize that these potential consequences do not absolve us of our responsibility to seek reconciliation. But we should seek wise counsel first. Particular wrongs call for particular counsel, so we do not wish to offer any blanket rules, beyond those offered by Jesus himself: seek reconciliation quickly, and let your yes be yes and your no be no. If you are unsure, consult with your sponsor and other godly individuals, including, if possible, your pastor. In short, do not foolishly rush into difficult amends, but do not foolishly avoid them, either.

STEP NINE
RECONCILIATION

So if you are offering your gift at the altar and there remember that your brother has something against you, leave your gift there before the altar and go. First be reconciled to your brother, and then come and offer your gift. Come to terms quickly with your accuser while you are going with him to court, lest your accuser hand you over to the judge, and the judge to the guard, and you be put in prison. Truly, I say to you, you will never get out until you have paid the last penny.

MATTHEW 5:23-26

As we begin to think about our amends, it is important to define what precisely an "amends" is. An "amends" is more than just an apology. An apology is an expression of regret. An amends is a compensation for a loss or injury, in the sense of attempting to "mend" the relationship and make things right. Its biblical equivalent is "reconciliation," which signifies a transformation or change.[32] In our case, the goal is to transform or change a broken relationship into a restored relationship. We do this by offering restitution, not just empty words.

It is hard to overemphasize the urgency of redressing the wrongs we have committed. If we remember that we have wronged our brother, we should drop whatever we are doing, even offering gifts to God, and seek reconciliation (Matthew 5:23-26). The point here, we think, is that we should never dally in making our amends. We should right our wrongs promptly and diligently, as if we were defendants seeking to avoid punishment.

This does not mean, however, that we should do so rashly or impulsively. The amends process is both exciting (when we want to be reconciled) and scary (when we don't), and so there is a real tendency to either jump the gun or drag our feet. Experience has taught us that we benefit from a careful and deliberate approach.

First, it is important to understand why we should make amends. Most obviously, we are commanded to do so, and it is clear that the consequences of not doing so are severe.[33] All sins are in fact sins against God (Psalm 51:4), and therefore we should address them promptly because we are commanded to be holy as God is holy (1 Peter 1:16). Moreover, we are also told to strive for peace with everyone (Hebrews 12:14a), particularly fellow members of the body (Romans 14:19), as an expression of God's

---

[32] *Cf.* 1 Corinthians 15:51-52.
[33] *See* Matthew 5:23-26.

love towards us (John 13:34). We simply cannot live peaceably without playing the role of peacemaker. Humbling ourselves before God and others can be unpleasant, but it is not optional.[34]

Second, it is important to understand how we should make amends. When we wrong others, our tendency is to say, "I'm sorry" and have that be the end of it. That is typically because we are not actually sorry. We don't regret what we have done; we regret the consequences of it. So, we apologize to make the consequences go away. Eventually, others catch on and our "apologies" stop having any effect. The biblical pattern, on the other hand, is that reconciliation doesn't come through empty words; it comes through repentance of sin and restitution. Repentance of sin comes from the heart, and recognizes that the behavior is the problem, not its consequences (2 Corinthians 7:9-10). It doesn't try to make excuses or shift blame. Similarly, restitution seeks to redress the consequences, not simply make them go away. If we owe money, we should return it (adding to what we owe as appropriate). If we have carelessly lost or damaged something, we should replace it. If we have stolen from someone, we should pay restitution.[35] When we go about our amends, we should keep these two principles in mind, acknowledging our regret and offering to make things right.

Next, we must ask to whom we should make amends. The short answer is anyone who has something against us. Christ does not limit his command to be reconciled, and neither should we. A good place to start is our inventory of our own resentments. If we are holding a grudge against someone else, chances are they are holding a grudge against us. We might then add anyone else we know we have harmed, provided they still have something against us. A good litmus test is this: "Do I feel agitated, tense, or guilty when I think about this person?" If so, we should probably make amends.

This test should not be used as an excuse to avoid amends. If we are already on good terms with the person, we might be tempted to think that an amends is not necessary. This, we think, is a mistake. Provided they have something against us, even a small thing, we should seek reconciliation. Our words have the power to heal or hurt, and so we should endeavor to use them to heal (Proverbs 18:21).

Typically, the longer we drag our feet in seeking reconciliation, the less likely we are to ever achieve it. The longer a wound festers, the more difficult it is to address. Moreover, out of fear we tend to delay the amends we most need to make. This, we think, is part of why the Bible puts so much stress on the urgency of reconciliation. Once we are prepared to make our amends, we should not waste any time. Christ

---

[34] *Cf.* James 4:9; 1 Pet 5:5-6; Phil 2:1-8.

[35] *Cf.* Exodus 22:1-17. Granted, as Christians we are not supposed to demand restitution from others (Matthew 5:38-39). However, we have no right to thereby absolve ourselves of our God-given responsibility to offer restitution.

tells us to seek reconciliation "quickly." How quickly? Before the sun goes down (Ephesians 4:26). We sinned with great urgency, and now we must bring this same urgency into our amends.

Experience has shown us that there is no excuse for procrastination. It may perhaps be impractical (though certainly not impossible!) to make all our amends in a single day, but it is not impractical to at least arrange them all in one day. Unless we have a list that is unusually long, most of us have found that we can easily find sufficient time within a day or two to contact everyone we need to contact to at least set up a time to meet or talk. The only real impediment to doing so is our own unwillingness.

As a preparatory action, we must arrange to make our amends. In doing so, we have found it helpful to reach out to the person and explain in a general way what we are trying to do, and ask them if they are able to spare the time (and if so, when). In doing so, we should aim for the mode of communication they are most likely to respond to. Thus, for instance, if they are unlikely to answer our calls, a written medium may be appropriate. We should be clear that this process is about us offering an unconditional apology and trying to make things right, not offering excuses or settling scores. We do not ask or expect anything in return.

As for making the amends itself, we would offer three concrete insights from our own experience.

First, if at all possible, amends should be done in-person, or if this is not possible, over the phone. Only as a last result should we use letters or e-mails. A letter or e-mail may be appropriate for arranging to make amends, but they are almost never appropriate for making one.

Second, when we make amends, we are cleaning up our own side of the street. The other party's behavior is simply not relevant to the task at hand. There might be a time to address the other party's sins, if any, but that time is not now.

Third, we should ask if there is anything we can do to make things right with them. Christ instructs us to be reconciled with others, not simply to apologize to them. To do so requires asking them what, if anything, we can do to achieve reconciliation. We should give them a chance to express their grievances, asking them to tell us if there is any other way we have harmed them.

Do not be surprised if someone does not respond to you immediately, or even if they respond poorly. It is easy to be offended, particularly if the other party is a Christian and therefore ought to be more forgiving. When confronted with this type of situation, we should ask ourselves whether we honestly tried to seek reconciliation.

If so, we have done what we can for now. We should ask God to provide another opportunity in his own time for us to be reconciled, and then wait patiently and prayerfully. It is a mistake, we think, to be pushy. It will help us to remember that some wounds run deep, and even if the other party does not forgive us, we know that God already has in Christ.

STEP NINE PRACTICAL APPLICATION

Ask for help. As with the other steps, the first thing we should do in preparing to make our amends is pray. We recommend asking God for three things in particular. First, ask God for the willingness to make the amends with speed, honesty, and forthrightness. Second, ask God to help you conduct yourself with wisdom, love, and contrition, being slow to speak, quick to admit fault, and clear-sighted and discerning. Third, ask God for help trusting his sovereign provision. Your job is to make the amends; God's job is to manage the results.

Act quickly. Everyone is afraid, at the outset, to make their amends. The longer we procrastinate, the worse this fear becomes. Therefore, we should not delay. Once we have our list and know what we plan to say, we should dive right in, preferably at a pace of at least one amends a day.

Follow up. Once we have made the amends, we must actually make the amends. Mouthing the right words is of no value if those words are not followed by action. Of course, we should be diligent to follow-through on any promises of restitution we have made. We must be people of our word (Matthew 5:37). But we must also follow up on changing the behaviors we are purporting to turn away from.

STEP TEN
MORTIFICATION

But that is not the way you learned Christ!—assuming that you have heard about him and were taught in him, as the truth is in Jesus, to put off your old self, which belongs to your former manner of life and is corrupt through deceitful desires, and to be renewed in the spirit of your minds, and to put on the new self, created after the likeness of God in true righteousness and holiness.

EPHESIANS 4:20-24

The preceding chapters have helped us lay a practical foundation for the rest of our lives. If we have been diligent in following instructions, we have made good progress. We have learned a good deal about ourselves, become familiar with some of the more useful tools in our spiritual toolkit, and even gotten a little bit of practice using them. But now comes the real work: fulfilling God's command to "work out your own salvation with fear and trembling" (Philippians 2:12). Our previous work may have been completed in only a few weeks, but this task will take us the rest of our lives.

As we prepare for this task, we should remember that we are living between two worlds. When we first believed, God granted us spiritual life. That is, he gave us a new spiritual nature that longs to trust, love, and obey him.[36] But in his wisdom, he did not completely remove our old sinful nature that longs to trust, love, and obey sin and the world. Thus, even though we have been born again, we have lurking inside of us a fortress where sin continues to prowl, in biblical terms called the "old man" or the "flesh," and from which sin is able to wage war against us. This indwelling sin clings close to us. It infects our thinking and desires. It resists the power of the Holy Spirit at work in us. In short, we may be free from sin, but we are not yet free of sin, because it continues to dwell in our flesh.[37]

Therefore, it is our duty to be perfecting our holiness, growing in grace and salvation, and renewing our inward man day by day.[38]

But how do we do this? **First**, we must continue to put off our old sinful nature, and **second**, we must continue to put on our new spiritual nature. This formula is the prescription for our spiritual development.[39]

---

[36] *Cf.* 2 Corinthians 5:17.

[37] *Cf.* Romans 7:13-23.

[38] *Cf.* 2 Corinthians 7:1; 1 Peter 2:2; 2 Peter 3:18; 2 Corinthians 4:16.

[39] *Cf.* Romans 8:13.

In the remaining three chapters, we will unpack this formula. In this chapter, we will discuss what it means to "put off" our old sinful nature (borrowing heavily from the Puritan classic *On the Mortification of Sin* by John Owen[40]). In Chapters 11 and 12, we will discuss what it means to "put on" our new spiritual nature.

So, to begin, what does it mean to put off or put to death the works of the flesh? It means to battle against sin. But our primary concern is not with our particular sins, but with our sinfulness and the flesh in which it resides, and only by extension any particular sins. Thus, the focus is on attacking our sinful tendencies and their stronghold, the flesh.

Before offering up a more precise definition, we should first understand what this putting off or putting to death of the flesh does not mean.

First, putting off the flesh does not mean the complete destruction of our sinful tendencies. This complete victory over sin will only occur when Christ returns in glory. If we think we have defeated our flesh or sinfulness, we are naively oblivious to our dangerous condition. Sinfulness is very much at work in our flesh, and will continue to be at work until we are taken up into glory.[41]

Second, putting off the flesh does not mean merely the renunciation of outward actions. Outward actions must be renounced, but sinfulness is a matter of our heart, and so we must address it at the heart level. If we correct the behavior without addressing the underlying cause, we are only whitewashing tombs.[42] We are just as sinful as we were before, but now we have added another sin on top of that: hypocrisy.

Third, putting off our flesh does not mean merely diverting sin to other outlets. It does us no good to renounce one sin if those sinful tendencies are diverted elsewhere, as when Simon the Magician gave up his sorceries only to have his covetousness manifest as greed.[43] Most of us have been able to effect change for a season by subordinating certain weaker desires to stronger desires, such as renouncing open drunkenness in service of our pride or ambition. But when we change one pattern of sin for another, we have merely changed the form of our slavery, not our slave-master (and in most cases, not for very long).

Fourth, putting off the flesh does not mean occasionally resisting our sins when they are particularly troublesome. Sin has a way of flaring up in our lives, either through a particularly powerful disturbance (such as a spree) or through a particularly painful consequence (such as damage to our relationships). In these instances, it is easy to

---

[40] John Owen, *On the Mortification of Sin in Believers* (1656).
[41] *Cf.* 1 John 3:2-4.
[42] *Cf.* Matthew 23:27-28.
[43] *See* Acts 8:9-24.

see and shrink back from our sins, and resolve to be done with them. This reaction is good, to be sure. These troubles are gifts from God, meant to bring us back to him for refuge and aid. But we must be sure we are reacting to the sin itself, not merely its consequences, or else we might be lying to God when we turn to him for deliverance. Eventually, the consequences go away, and when they do, all too often so does our resolve to put off the flesh and battle against our sin.

Having established what putting off the flesh does not mean, what does it mean, stated positively? It means to **systematically and relentlessly battle against the habitual inclination and bent of the will and affections toward engaging in particular sins**.[44] In other words, putting off the flesh is our battle against the lusts that cause our sins, *i.e.*, our sinfulness.[45] It is moving beyond the fruit and taking the ax to the root of the tree.

As the definition suggests, this process should be **systematic**. As fallen creatures, our old natures are not only evil, they are also deceitful.[46] In setting out to put these sinful natures to death, we must be wary of our adversary. Our sinfulness will try to hide from us, to masquerade as other things, to fool us into underestimating its power. Our sinfulness is systematically working to destroy us, and therefore we must be systematic in our work to destroy it. Otherwise, it will inevitably gain the upper hand.

Furthermore, this process should be **relentless**. Knowing that we will never be entirely rid of our sin, we should constantly fight to weaken it. Our experience tells us that just because a lust is quiet does not mean it is dead. We should bring the same vigilance to putting off all our sinfulness, even when a particular lust is not producing any particular fruit. It is not for nothing that the Christian walk is compared to spiritual warfare.[47] If you gain an advantage over a particular lust, good: exploit that advantage to rout your enemy.

In sum, we should have a process for combatting sin (systematic) that we try to follow every day whether things are going well or poorly (relentless). So, what does this look like?

RESISTING TEMPTATION

First, we should have a plan in place to resist sin in the moment, and in doing so be diligent in our efforts not to gratify the desires of our flesh.

---

[44] Cf. John Owen, *On the Mortification of Sin in Believers*, Chapter VI, Section 2 (1656).
[45] *See* James 1:14-15.
[46] *See* Ecclesiastes 8:11, Jeremiah 17:9.
[47] *See* Ephesians 6:11-17

We must put off the old man by putting off his practices. We must not present our members to sin as instruments of unrighteousness. It is tempting to think that if we give into temptation a little bit, we will be less tempted to sin. In fact, we find the opposite to be true. There is no "pressure valve" in our hearts that allows us to release the pressure of temptation through sinning. All that sinning accomplishes is strengthening our lusts. It is the same as giving our sinfulness the weapons and material it needs to fortify its position and more effectively reap destruction. In the interest of keeping things simple, we suggest a three-step process for resisting temptation in the moment:

First, we ask God to remove the temptation. God desires our holiness, and desires to grant it to us. So, if we are diligent, persistent, and sincere in asking for his aid, he will give it. His grace is greater than all our sin.

Second, we rehearse to ourselves the goodness of God and his true promises and the vileness of sin and its false promises. We remind ourselves of all the times sin has over promised and under delivered, and we remind ourselves of all the times God has been faithful to us despite our weakness.

Third, we promptly turn our thoughts to someone we can help. As will be addressed more fully in Chapters 11 and 12, the best way to weaken the desires of the flesh is to walk in step with the Spirit. If we humbly focus on how best to love and serve others, we will find our thoughts drawn back to Christ and away from temptation.

If we follow this formula, we can break the power of temptation—God will not let you be tempted beyond your ability, and will always provide a way of enduring or escaping (1 Corinthians 10:13). We must begin to train ourselves to turn to God in prayer whenever we are tempted to sin, asking him to remove the temptation and empower us with his Spirit. Soon, this practice will become a habit.

UPROOTING SIN

Second, we must begin to take the ax to the tree. As we said earlier, our problem is not particular sins, but rather the sinfulness that dwells in our fallen hearts. Uprooting sin requires that we search out our sinfulness and its stronghold, and then we attack.

How do we search out our sinfulness? Using the same methods we have already learned in Chapters 4 through 9, every day.

First, we ask ourselves why we sinned—that is, we inventory our sin to identify the heart idols that are driving it. We sin because our desires are at war within us.

And therefore, if we seek to understand the workings of our sin, we must seek to understand the workings of our idolatrous desires. Toward this end, we recommend keeping a running inventory, similar to what we prepared in Chapter 4, at the end of every day, not just for the original categories listed, but also for other situations that crop up—such as an argument with a spouse or a recurring sinful behavior. This ongoing inventory will help us understand ourselves better, and the twists and turns our fallen nature takes over time.

But above all, we should be diligent with this process. If we are not, we may find that resentments and other troubles add up once again.

Second, we confess it to God and to others—that is, we acknowledge our wrong and seek accountability. If we confess our sin to God he will supply us with his grace and forgiveness. If we confess our sin to others, they can comfort us, pray for us, and exhort us to greater holiness.

Third, we humbly ask God to change us—that is, we approach him in humility and ask him to reshape the desires of our hearts. God alone has the power to produce lasting change, and so our only hope of deliverance from sin is the power of God. Luckily for us, we know that he will bring to completion the work that he has begun in us,[48] and therefore we can approach him with confidence.

Fourth, to the extent that we have harmed others, we promptly make amends— that is, we continue to live out Christ's command to seek reconciliation. We do so promptly and without reference to the other party's harm. Our job is to address the log in our own eye, not the speck in our brother's.

In this way, we are able to begin to routinely and relentlessly expose the deceitfulness of sin and retrain our affections. It may not produce noticeable results on a day-to-day basis, but over time, we will begin to love God more fully and hate sin more fiercely because God's beauty and sin's ugliness will become clearer to us. As our love for God grows and our love for sin begins to weaken, we will find freedom from the power of sin.

This chapter is by no means a complete account of how we can go about putting off our flesh. But it gives us enough to begin the task. In the next chapter, we will begin to address the other side of the formula: how to "put on" the new man.

STEP TEN PRACTICAL APPLICATION

Continue to ask God for help. Whenever we catch ourselves slipping into sin, we at

---

[48] *Cf.* Philippians 1:6

once ask God to deliver us from temptation and remove any sinful desires at play. We then promptly turn our thoughts to how to serve others. Do not give your sin time to fester.

Continue to take inventory. We continue to take stock of our emotions (particularly anger, fear, and lust) and watch for sinful behavior, both throughout the day and at the end of the day. At night, we prepare a written inventory, which we have found is more effective than a mental inventory in terms of helping us recognize our part and admit it to God. We have provided some example inventories in **Appendix B**. The most important thing is consistency: if we build a habit of watchfulness and self-examination, then we will be well served in our battle against the flesh. In order to build such a habit, we recommend taking a nightly inventory every night for 90 days.

Continue to acknowledge and set right our sins. God's commands to acknowledge our sins and be reconciled to others have no expiration date. As we continue to sin, we continue to acknowledge our sins to God and to others (sponsors, small-group members, spouse, etc.) and continue to try to set right any wrongs we commit. At first, these practices are strange and difficult, but in time they will become routine and easy.

STEP ELEVEN
PRAYER AND MEDITATION

Therefore, as you received Christ Jesus the Lord, so walk in him, rooted and built up in him and established in the faith, just as you were taught, abounding in thanksgiving.

COLOSSIANS 2:6-7

In Chapter 10, we discussed the two-part formula for Christian growth—**first**, we must continue to put off our old sinful nature, and **second**, we must continue put on our new spiritual nature—and discussed what it means to "put off" our sinful nature.

In Chapters 11 and 12, we will discuss what it means to "put on" our new spiritual nature. At its most basic, it can be summarized as follows: "as you received Christ Jesus the Lord, so walk in him" (Colossians 2:6). In other words, we received Christ through the Spirit by hearing with faith, and so we should continue in him in that same way.[49]

But what does this mean? Two things: (1) set your mind on the things above, and (2) walk according to the Spirit. In this chapter, we will work through what it means to set our minds on the things above. In Chapter 12, we will work through what it means to walk according to the Spirit.

To begin with, the command:

If then you have been raised with Christ, seek the things that are above, where Christ is, seated at the right hand of God. Set your minds on things that are above, not on things that are on earth. For you have died, and your life is hidden with Christ in God. When Christ who is your life appears, then you also will appear with him in glory.

COLOSSIANS 3:1-4

In living out this command, we suggest two practical areas of focus: meditation and prayer.

MEDITATION

What is meditation as a Christian? It is not, per modern practice, emptying one's mind, but rather the opposite: it is filling one's mind by setting it on the things that are above! As Paul says, we should "let the word of Christ dwell in [us] richly" through teaching, admonishment, and song (Colossians 3:16).

---

[49] *Cf.* Galatians 3:1-6.

When we hear "word of Christ" or "word of God," we think of the Bible. And this is part of it. But the Bible uses the term more broadly to refer to the whole teaching of God.

Therefore, the command to let the word of Christ dwell in us is of course a command to read the Bible. But it is also a command to attend to the word of God preached from the pulpit.[50] It is also a command to attend to the word of God when preached by our brothers and sisters in Christ. Lastly, it is a command to attend to the word of Christ as sung in music. Christianity is a singing religion, and we are explicitly commanded to sing God's praises throughout the Bible.[51]

Towards this end, we suggest three practical meditative disciplines:

Meditative Discipline #1: Bible Reading

We should make a habit of regularly reading the Bible. Our goal here should be two-fold:

First, we should read the Bible for its content. The Bible is God's word to us for our edification, and will be the primary means by which he communicates his will to us. Towards this end, we suggest developing a habit of reading at least 3-4 chapters every day, with a goal of completing the entire book in a year. Once that is done, we recommend starting over again! In this way, God's word will grow to permeate our thinking and guide our actions as we learn to discern what is good and acceptable and perfect in his eyes.

Second, we should apply it to our lives. We should aim to be doers of the word and not hearers only. So, we should aim to apply what we read. As a beginning point, we suggest asking some simple questions about what we've read:

- Does it address a sin I am committing and should repent of?

- Does it address a command that I should obey?

- Does it address a promise I should trust?

- Does it address a doctrine I should believe or avoid?

- Does it address an example I should follow or avoid?

We suggest keeping a journal in which to jot down our answers. This not only helps us keep track of what we learn, it also keeps us focused. In this way, we aim to let God teach and admonish us through his word and Spirit.

---

[50] *See* 1 Thessalonians 2:13, Romans 10:17.
[51] *See* Psalm 150.

Meditative Discipline #2: Submitting to Teaching

We should make a habit of regularly submitting to sound teaching. This comes in three primary forms:

First, we should regularly attend gatherings in which the word of God is faithfully preached. The precise style of preaching is less important than that we diligently seek to hear and apply it with a soft heart. We recognize that no human, even a minister of the word, is free of error when they speak, and they should not be treated as such. But we have nonetheless found it helpful to allow preachers to clearly proclaim the word in a way that appeals to our spirit and stirs up our affections for God and his truth.

Second, we should seek out supplementary teaching. For some, this means attending classes offered by their church. For others, it means listening to seminary courses or other preachers. For still others, it means reading books on Christian theology and practice. Whatever the form, the principle is the same: we should take advantage of the available resources to grow in our understanding of God.

Last, we should involve ourselves in a smaller group seeking to live out God's salvation. We do this because it is very easy to slip into a sterile Christian life wherein we focus on having the right answers, rather than applying what we know in love. Our posture in these small groups should not be primarily as a teacher of others. Yes, we should seek to serve others by speaking truth in love when appropriate. But our primary goal in these groups should be to love others and allow them to teach, exhort, admonish, and edify us. In short, we should seek out small group fellowship to allow others to help us apply what we've learned to our own lives.

Meditative Discipline #3: Song

The last meditative discipline we suggest is song. While song is not traditionally considered a meditative discipline, Paul groups it together with teaching and admonishment (Colossians 3:16). Therefore, we suggest cultivating a habit of singing hymns, and psalms, and spiritual songs. There are two easy ways to do this:

First, we should sing in gathered worship. For some, especially newer Christians, this can feel awkward—particularly if we do not yet know the songs. And yet it is commanded. So, our suggestion is to simply start singing. Once we started, we found it became easier.

Second, we should sing on our own time. Whether we do this in our own family worship time, during our commute, or throughout the day, we should look for opportunities to expose our hearts with spiritual music that appeals to us—and sing along. Simply put, doing so will help draw our hearts Godward.

PRAYER

If meditation is half of what it means to seek the things that are above, prayer is the other half.

In particular, prayer is an acknowledgment of the centrality of God. Not only is God the most important thing, but that all other good things come from God, and without him, nothing we do will succeed (Psalm 127:1). If indeed God is sovereign over all things and has promised to answer our prayers, it would be foolish not to praise him and seek his aid in prayer.

From this, two questions arise: "How should we pray?" and "What should we pray?"

First, the how.

We should pray simply.[52] We should not babble like the pagans do, or think that through our eloquence that God will show us favor. Rather, God already knows what we need—so all we need to do is ask and ask simply.

We should pray constantly.[53] God is present in all situations, and therefore prayer is appropriate in every situation, no matter how mundane. When we experience joy, we should praise him. When tested, we should flee to him. When suffering, we should seek refuge in him. When in difficult circumstances, we should petition him for aid. We should ask him for help at work, we should praise him while enjoying a walk in the park, etc. There is no situation in which it is not appropriate to seek God in prayer.

We should pray persistently.[54] Just because God did not answer our prayer immediately does not mean he does not want to grant it. Indeed, we know that he wants to give us every good gift. But he also wants us to learn persistence, to continue to return to him for aid. Thus, in his wisdom, he will sometimes delay giving us what we ask for to teach us patience and persistence, and so our part is to continue asking.

We should avoid praying to be seen by others.[55] Here we do not think that the primary emphasis is on praying in secret (though that is a good habit to cultivate), but rather on the motivations behind our prayers. It is clear from the ministry of Jesus and his apostles that there is a place for public or communal prayer, but even when we are praying in a group, we should guard ourselves against the temptation to pray for the purpose of being recognized by others for our wisdom, eloquence, and godliness. Prayer is for God, not for others.

---

[52] *See* Matthew 6:7.
[53] *See* 1 Thessalonians 5:17.
[54] *See* Luke 18:1-8.
[55] *See* Matthew 6:5-6.

We should pray expectantly.[56] God has promised to give us whatever good thing we ask for in Christ's name. So, if we desire something good (that is, it is good for us) and we ask for it in Christ's name (that is, to glory Christ and not simply to gratify our passions), we should ask and expect to receive it. But we should also be careful to acknowledge that God has a much better picture of what is good for us than we do, and so if God does not answer our prayer, we should praise him all the more.

With these points in mind, we suggest cultivating a simple practice of prayer. We should make prayer a priority and allot time to it, at least twice a day (morning and evening), as well as throughout the day. As with most disciplines, if we don't make time for prayer, it won't happen.

We should also be vigilant against dead routine. It is easy for our "quiet time" to become a ritual action, rather than a genuine motivation of our heart. In this case, we are dishonoring God because we hypocritically honor him with our lips while our hearts are far from him. God desires our hearts, not our external observance.[57] It is equally easy to slip into a time of self-directed reflection or stillness, completely devoid of any need for God. If so, our quiet time will become sterile silence, because God, not quiet, is the driver of our spiritual growth.

Second, the what.

Jesus gives us a simple example of what we should pray for:

> *"Our Father in heaven, hallowed be your name. Your kingdom come, your will be done, on earth as it is in heaven. Give us this day our daily bread, and forgive us our debts, as we also have forgiven our debtors. And lead us not into temptation, but deliver us from evil."*
>
> MATTHEW 6:9-13

First, we should praise God and give thanks to him ("hallowed be your name").[58] God is ultimate goodness, and the source of all other goodness. Therefore, we should be quick to praise him and give thanks to him for all the good things we have. In this way, we remind our souls to be satisfied in him, and to be thankful for his provision.

Second, we should pray for the advance of his kingdom ("Your kingdom come, your will be done, on earth as it is in heaven"). We are living out a cosmic struggle between good and evil, between the kingdom of God and the kingdom of Satan. We know who will be victorious, but there is much work to be done—any many souls to be saved—between now and the end of the age, when Christ returns in glory. It is easy

---

[56] *See* John 14:13 and 1 John 5:14.
[57] *Cf.* Matthew 9:13.
[58] *See* Psalm 100, 118, 136.

to lose track of this reality and get caught up in the minutia of our day-to-day lives, but the most important thing for us and for the world is the advancement of God's kingdom, in our own hearts and the hearts of others. Therefore, we should ask God to advance his kingdom through revival in our churches and communities, success in our evangelism, and effectiveness in our ministries.

Third, we should ask God to provide for us ("Give us this day our daily bread"). We are material creatures, and we have material needs and wants. We should therefore ask God to provide for those needs and wants, understanding that he will provide exactly what we need, if not exactly what we want.

Fourth, we should ask God for forgiveness ("forgive us our debts"). We have been cleansed once for all by the blood of Christ, and yet we are still called to acknowledge our sin and seek forgiveness from him. In doing so, we will find spiritual healing and fuel our spiritual growth. Therefore, we should be quick to confess our wrongdoing and ask him for forgiveness.

Fifth, we should intercede for others ("as we also have forgiven our debtors"). The Bible is quite clear that we should pray not only for our friends and loved ones, but also for our enemies. We should pray for unbelievers that God would open doors for us to share the gospel and open their hearts to believe it. We should pray for believers that they would grow in the grace of Jesus and grow closer to God. We should pray for those who are hurting and mourning, and praise God for those who are rejoicing. We suggest keeping a list of people and making a habit of regularly including them and their needs in our prayers.

Sixth, we should pray for spiritual protection ("lead us not into temptation"). Stated negatively, we should ask God to help us avoid falling into sin. Thus, if we find ourselves tempted, we should ask him to remove the temptation and weaken its power over our hearts. Stated positively, we should ask God to grow us and conform us to the image of his Son, strengthening us particularly in areas where we are weak.

Lastly, we should pray for deliverance ("but deliver us from evil"). God is our refuge and our deliverer, in good times as well as bad. He watches over and protects us, even in difficult circumstances. If we find ourselves struggling with our circumstances, we should ask God to deliver us from those circumstances (if it is his will to do so) and strengthen, protect, and grow us to be faithful in them (if it is not).

Practically speaking, we can emulate the prayer pattern that Christ Jesus gave us by working through these categories using the Lord's Prayer as an aid, praying for things that come to mind for each. In the beginning, this method might seem overly mechanical, but it will help us learn the building blocks of biblical prayer, which is the bedrock of a well-rounded prayer life.

STEP ELEVEN PRACTICAL APPLICATION

In terms of putting these commands into practice quickly, we recommend the following:

Meditate on God and his glory. By this we mean three things. First, we should set our minds on God's goodness and glory and the better hope that awaits us. Practically, we recommend setting aside time each day to read the Bible and reflect on Christ and his work, the grace God has shown you, the promises of God and how they have been fulfilled in our lives, and of course his glory.

Second, we should diligently seek out resources for our teaching and instruction, both in our local church as well as supplemental materials such as books and recordings. Time permitting, you might get involved in a Bible study or similar meeting dedicated to understanding and applying God's word in your life.

Third, we should make it a priority to sing God's praises, especially in gathered worship but also at other times.

Pray! Immediately begin to set aside time for prayer every day, at least twice a day. If we have not already built this habit, it is now time to start. The way you build this habit is to be habitual about it—try not to miss even a single day. If we are not consistent in prayer, we cannot expect consistent spiritual growth. If you do not know what to pray for, ask for help praying, and try to adapt (not merely recite) one of the many examples provided in Scripture, particularly the Lord's Prayer.

An important note about spiritual disciplines: they are a means to an end, not an end in themselves. The goal of these disciplines is to help us build a relationship with God—to seek him, to know him better, to find comfort in him, and to grow in him. Without God, they are of no intrinsic value. We are not made holy by our meditation or prayers. Rather, through our meditations and prayers we hope to grow closer to the God who has already made us holy and continues to make us holier day by day.

STEP TWELVE
SPONSORSHIP

Now the eleven disciples went to Galilee, to the mountain to which Jesus had directed them. And when they saw him they worshiped him, but some doubted. And Jesus came and said to them, "All authority in heaven and on earth has been given to me. Go therefore and make disciples of all nations, baptizing them in the name of the Father and of the Son and of the Holy Spirit, teaching them to observe all that I have commanded you. And behold, I am with you always, to the end of the age."

MATTHEW 28:16-20

In Chapter 10 and 11, we discussed the two-part formula for Christian growth—**first**, we must continue to put off our old sinful nature, and **second**, we must continue to put on our new spiritual nature—and discussed what it means to "put off" our sinful nature. Further, we discussed how to "put on" on new spiritual nature by (1) setting our minds on the things above, and (2) walking according to the Spirit. In Chapter 11, we worked through what it means to set our minds on the things above. In this chapter, we will work through what it means to walk according to the Spirit.

So, what does it mean to walk according to the Spirit? It means to obey God's statutes and rules (*i.e.*, to love God and love others), according to the power of the Holy Spirit which God has given to us:

And I will give you a new heart, and a new spirit I will put within you. And I will remove the heart of stone from your flesh and give you a heart of flesh. And I will put my Spirit within you, and cause you to walk in my statutes and be careful to obey my rules.

EZEKIEL 36:26-27

In short, it means not simply outward conformity of our actions to God's rules, but inward conformity of our hearts through the transformative power of the Spirit.[59] As the Spirit transforms our hearts to overflow with love, joy, peace, patience, kindness, goodness, faithfulness, gentleness, and self-control, we will find ourselves becoming more obedient to God, provided we cooperate with his work. This begins (per Chapter 11) with setting our minds on the things of the Spirit, and ends with living according to the Spirit and obeying him in the form of "putting on" these new heart attributes. In short, we are cooperatively working out through our actions what God is working in our hearts through his Spirit.[60]

---

[59] *Cf.* Romans 8:5-9.
[60] *Cf.* Philippians 2:12-13; Colossians 3:12-15.

Thus, if we wish to grow spiritually, we should seek out ways to "put on" Christ. Obviously, there will be opportunities to do so throughout the day, and when God prepares good works for us to walk in, we should seize these as gifts from God. But we have also found it helpful to deliberately seek out some kind of commitment to serve, and make ourselves available through that.

The task of "putting on" Christ can take an endless number of shapes and takes a lifetime of work, and therefore detailing it in its fullness is well beyond the scope of this book. Instead, we wish to focus on one of the simplest and most fitting ways to "put on" Christ, which is to lovingly and patiently pass along what was so freely given to us.

The end goal of the program outlined in this book is to advance the Kingdom of God for the glory of God. We hope to do this in two ways. First, we hope to help spiritually sick people find spiritual health by submitting to the reign and rule of Jesus Christ. Second, we hope to show those same people how to help the next person.

Therefore, once we finish working through the steps, we should begin to "sponsor" others. Someone took the time to help us find freedom in our lives, and now we should pay it forward to others as they seek to do the same.

The most common objection to sponsorship is that people feel they are not qualified to help others. Luckily, we have found that this is usually not the case.

First of all, sponsorship is straightforward. You would indeed be unqualified if your job as sponsor were to help fix other people through sage advice. But luckily for you, your job is simpler than that. Your job as sponsor is to simply help guide your sponsee through the process as quickly as possible, providing them some basic guidance and accountability along the way. In other words, you don't liberate them from sin—God does. So, let God do the work, using the tools outlined in these steps.

Think of this process as a spiritual training program using methods that are set out in the Bible. Someone else has already developed and organized it for you; all you need to do is help your sponsee follow it. You don't need to be an expert theologian to tell a sponsee to trust God, examine his heart, and help others. All you need to do is show your sponsee how to work the steps, just like your sponsor showed you.

Second, don't underestimate your usefulness. Your past experiences with particular patterns of sin have equipped you to be of particular service to others struggling with the same types of sin. God will use you to reach them in ways that others might not be able to. Therefore, we encourage you to make yourself available to them.

If you still have fears, you should just start doing it. You will soon discover that it is easier than you think. More than that, there is great joy and satisfaction to be found in helping others as others have helped you.

FINDING SPONSEES

To start with, finding sponsees is an active process, not a passive one. It is your responsibility to seek out new sponsees, and to broach the topic of sponsorship with them. We suggest that you set aside a dedicated time each week to attend meetings where you might run into newcomers who need help.

When you've found a newcomer, be welcoming and pursue them. You don't need to (nor should you necessarily) ask them to let you sponsor them. But you should at least let them know that you are willing to do so. It is okay to let them ask you, but it is a difficult thing for a newcomer to ask someone to be their sponsor, so make it easy for them.

DISCUSSING SPONSORSHIP WITH A POTENTIAL SPONSEE

When someone asks you to sponsor him or her, we suggest that you take thirty minutes or so to better understand him or her, and to frankly outline the process.

First things first: try to learn more about your prospective sponsee. Figure out what she wants help with and why. Ask about her spiritual background. Ask about what other solutions she's tried in the past. These questions will help you better relate to her. But most importantly, inquire as to whether she is a Christian—that is, whether she believes that Jesus is the Christ, the Son of God, who died for our sins and was raised for our justification, and she has trusted in him for salvation. If not, then evangelism should be your priority.

Once you've gotten a better understanding of your prospective sponsee, you should explain that this program is designed for people who want to break free of a particular sinful behavior, not merely manage it. In other words, complete abstinence from that particular sinful behavior is what we hope to achieve (though admittedly there may be some backsliding along the way). We have found that trying to control, rather than eliminate, sinful behavior is ineffective. In many instances, it is affirmatively harmful. If a prospective sponsee has not yet arrived at the conclusion that she must stop completely, then the program outlined in this book will be of little value to her. Counseling is a more appropriate solution in that kind of situation, and you are not qualified to do that.

This instruction should not be read to mean that a sponsee cannot have any doubts, reservations, or uncertainty. No one is ever entirely ready to be rid of sin. Rather, we hope to be clear about what is expected, while also being careful not to slip into condescension or self-righteousness. When you make yourself available, do so in a spirit of humility, not arrogance. We are just beggars showing other beggars where we found bread. In all things, we should act with truth, love, and gentleness.

Next, you should outline the process in detail. Start by explaining the twelve steps. Explain exactly what you did, focusing particularly on steps four and five and step nine (the ones people tend to balk at). In doing this, the goal is to help your prospective sponsee "count the cost" of what she is getting into. When you have finished explaining the twelve steps, explain the process: you will read through this book together and whenever you come across a suggestion, he or she will be expected to take that suggestion. And then, when you are finished with the steps, your sponsee will be expected to help others in the same way you have helped him or her.

Lastly, you should explain that this is a God-centered program. What that means is that every suggestion in this book is of no value on its own. Similarly, you as a sponsor are not going to save your sponsee. Only God can do that. The purpose of this book, and your purpose as sponsor, is to point your sponsee towards a deeper, more personal relationship with God.

WORKING STEP-BY-STEP

Assuming your prospective sponsee is willing to go through the process, we suggest you begin to meet with him or her once a week. If you'd like, feel free to give your sponsee the "homework" of reading the chapter carefully before you meet. At the outset, we suggest a pace of at least one chapter (one step) per week, reading through the book together, following any suggestions, sharing your own experience, answering any questions, etc. It is more important to get through the first three steps quickly than it is to pedantically hammer home every last point of theology in the first three chapters. As long as she understands the gospel, she understands everything she needs to know to continue. Furthermore, it is always appropriate to refer back to earlier chapters for clarifications and reminders when applicable.

When you arrive at the fourth step, you will have to set aside several weeks for your sponsee to prepare inventories. There are two basic approaches to the inventory process, and we have had success with both. One approach gives the sponsee two weeks to complete all three inventories. Two weeks is more than enough time to do it—assuming they are willing. The other approach has them prepare the inventories one column per week (columns 1 & 2 of the resentment inventory in week one, column 3 in week two, column 4 in week three; columns 1 & 2 of the fear inventory in week one, etc.) with periodic check-ins about how things are coming and what they are seeing. Feel free to use either approach (or tailor the approach to your specific sponsee).

Sponsees tend to get bogged down in step four. Don't be too concerned or surprised if that happens. Just keep encouraging them to work at it, and wait to continue on with the work until they are done. Sometimes sponsees decide they would rather not continue with the process. If that happens, don't beat yourself up. Just wish them the best and continue to pray for them.

Once the fourth step is finished, continue to proceed at a pace of one chapter per week until you reach step nine.

As with step four, you will need to set aside a few weeks for amends. As outlined in this book, we suggest making amends at a rate of at least one a day. This pace is easily achievable—if the sponsee is willing to do it. Some sponsees need a little more prodding than others, though, so keep being patient and encouraging. Honestly facing up to the past can be intimidating. If your sponsee can't make an amends to a particular person for a good reason, it's okay to tell her to wait until the opportunity presents itself. Simply communicate that when the opportunity does present itself, she should address it urgently, in keeping with what Jesus taught about reconciliation. As with step four, do not continue working the steps until your sponsee is finished making those amends she can currently make.

Once your sponsee has made all the amends she can reasonably make, continue on at a pace of one chapter per week until you have finished.

Of course, this timeline is only a rough guide based on our own experience. It won't fit every case. Do not feel obligated to follow it to the letter. If you need to adapt something or if you think your sponsee would benefit from more (or less!) time, use your best judgment.

Similarly, the process outlined in this book is just that—an outline. It is not the Bible and it is not a substitute for a Spirit-led believer exercising wisdom and discernment in love. Therefore, do not feel bound to do everything exactly the way it is outlined herein. This book is about spiritual principles, not legalistic rules. The only word of caution is that these methods have been very effective for us in the past, so if you are going to make changes, make sure you do so with wisdom, humility, and love. In other words, only make changes for a good reason—particularly if you are inexperienced with taking others through the process. It is easy to slip into the trap of thinking we have all the answers and making changes for the sake of making changes. Years of experience have taught us that these sorts of changes are usually for the worse, not the better.

ANSWERING QUESTIONS AND GIVING COUNSEL

Your sponsee will, from time to time, run into problems or seek counsel about other issues besides step work (relationship troubles, work conflicts, etc.).

Try to approach these situations with care and humility. In particular, remember that you are her sponsor, not her counselor, therapist, pastor, or lawyer. You are a process manager. Your job, as a sponsor, is to teach her to rely upon the tools God has provided, not to rely upon you as a sponsor. So, if a sponsee calls asking for advice with a difficult situation, point her to the tools outlined in this book.

Specifically, we suggest pointing your sponsee to five tools that are effective in almost every difficult situation:

Ask God for clarity and strength. The very first thing we should do is ask God for the discernment to see the situation clearly and the strength to resist the pull towards sin. Humble reliance upon God is the cornerstone of spiritual transformation.

Inventory the problem. If we are upset or engaged in some kind of sin, we take a quick inventory of the problem (mental or written). Using the tools outlined in this book, we try to get to the heart of the issue. If your sponsee has not yet finished the fourth step, coach him or her through a basic inventory.

Turn your thoughts to God and others. Once we've done that, we try to deliberately turn our thoughts to God and to others. We ask ourselves how we can show our love for God through obedience in this situation and how we can show our love for others by humbly serving them. Even simple things (turning back to your work, calling someone new, etc.) can be of great benefit in snapping us out of our self-centeredness.

Study the Bible. Given that the Bible is God's word, it is the first place we should go for answers. It addresses every situation we will find ourselves in, either directly or indirectly. We just need to know where to look. Often, a quick internet search will turn up the answer (e.g. "bible verses about employers"). Other times, we might need to ask a pastor or mentor.

Seek out wise counsel. Lastly, armed with a better understanding of the problem, we take the issue to other Christians whose counsel we trust. As a general rule, we recommend seeking out counsel from people other than our sponsor. God has given us a whole community of wise and godly people, so we should not learn to rely on only one.

In this way, we will begin to train our sponsees in a process that will allow him or her to rely upon God and his grace rather than upon you.

AFTER COMPLETING THE STEPS

Assuming you have diligently followed the directions set out in this book, once your sponsee is finished with this chapter, your work as her sponsor is formally finished and she is ready to start sponsoring others.

Just because your work as her sponsor is finished doesn't mean the relationship is over. Make it clear that you will still be available to meet or answer questions as things crop up. But don't feel obligated to continue meeting once a week unless your sponsee requests it. Part of the goal here is to help your sponsee learn to rely upon God and his grace rather than advice and accountability from you.

MEETINGS

Encourage your sponsee (and yourself, for that matter) to regularly attend several meetings a week, at least in the beginning. "Meeting makers make it," the saying goes. Meetings and fellowship are an indispensable part of the twelve-step process. People who make meetings tend to see spiritual fruit. People who don't make meetings tend to fall back into patterns of sin. It is as simple as that. God has made us to exist in fellowship, and meetings are a good form of fellowship.

However, this should not be read to mean that meetings are a substitute for the steps. They are not. But by the same token, the steps are not a substitute for meetings. Fellowship and action go hand-in-hand. Both are necessary components of spiritual fitness.

So how do we "make meetings"?

First, we have to **find** meetings. If you don't already know of a handful of Christ-centered twelve-step meetings, ask your sponsor or your pastor for help. Celebrate Recovery® is probably the most common, but many churches have their own programs. There are also many non-Christian twelve-step meetings, depending on the precise issues with which you struggle. These meetings can be helpful as well, provided you stick to the basics (trust God, clean house, help others) and avoid getting too deep into theology. There are always church groups to be involved in that provide community and accountability. If all else fails, we can start our own twelve-step meeting and try to find fellow sufferers to join us.

Second, we have to **attend** meetings. At a bare minimum, we should be able to make it to one or two meetings a week. We commonly claim that we "don't have time" to make meetings. Experience shows that this is simply not the case. For someone who is serious about getting better, there is always time to make at least one meeting a day and several meetings a week. If we can't find the time, it is just a matter of making time and making it a priority.

Third, we **make the most** of meetings. We show up early and try to talk to others. We seek out people who need our help. We exchange contact information. We share honestly (even if all we can honestly say is that we don't want to be there). We listen attentively to and pray for others. And, perhaps most importantly, we stay for the "meeting after the meeting," when people hang around talking or go to dinner—often we will learn more about living godly lives in the hour after the meeting than during the meeting itself.

In short, be diligent to make meetings. By doing so, you will begin to find fellowship of like-minded fellow sufferers and you can all mutually help point one another to Jesus in times of difficulty.

AVOIDING COMMON PROBLEMS

Sponsorship is simple, but it is not always easy. The work of trying to help fellow sufferers can be exhilarating, but it can also be frustrating. Many problems await unwary sponsors who do not understand their own need for Jesus or their own role in the process. We would like to highlight five in particular, from our own experience:

Self-Righteousness. The most common problem sponsors run into is self-righteousness. They believe that because they worked the steps, they have the right to pass judgment or feel superior to those who have not—or will not. Not only is this attitude thoughtless—like the servant who was forgiven a great debt but refused to forgive a far lesser debt he is owed[61]—it is spiritually toxic. We are all fellow servants of Christ, and before our own master we will stand or fall. We have no right to pass judgment on Christ's servants.

Codependency. We, as sponsors, have no ability to fix someone else. All we can do is point them to God and pray that God heals them. All too frequently, though, sponsors slip into an unhealthy pattern of "enabling" their sponsees to sin by shielding them or helping them avoid the consequences of that sin. Worse yet, they let their own sense of worth get tied up with the success or failure of their sponsees, going to greater and greater lengths to "help" those sponsees and beating themselves up when they fail. At its root, this attitude is one of pride. We forget that God is the one who fixes others, and begin to play God ourselves.

---

[61] *Cf.* Matthew 18:21-35.

Harshness. If codependency is one extreme in sponsorship, then harshness is the other. Sometimes, after being burned by codependent behavior towards sponsees, we adopt unloving or unmerciful attitudes towards our sponsees. We detach from them completely, bullying them into working the steps and washing our hands of them if they don't. We tell ourselves that all we are there to do is point them to God, and thereby absolve ourselves of our God-given responsibility to show love, compassion, and mercy to others.

Legalism. There is a very thin line between using the steps as a rigorous spiritual training program designed to lead us into a deeper relationship with God, on the one hand, and using the steps as a system of rules we use to control our spiritual life and avoid God entirely. The former is grace-infused obedience, the latter is legalism. The former recognizes God as the Alpha and the Omega of our spiritual life and merely seeks to help us obey him more fully. The latter treats the steps as the center of our spiritual life, and God as a useful add-on. Twelve-step recovery programs are littered with souls of people who have forgotten that the steps are only a means to God—not an end in themselves. The steps will not save you or your sponsee. Only God can do that.

Idolatry. For those of us who have had their spiritual outlook changed by this process, it is easy to slip into a sort of idolatry around the steps. "The steps changed my life" quickly becomes "the steps are the key to spiritual growth," which in turn becomes "the steps are how you find God," and lastly, "the steps are the thing to which I give glory rather than God." We seldom vocalize this last sentiment, but it is nonetheless quite common. The steps are nothing more than a useful tool: they are a systematic and methodical way of applying God's spiritual principles and practices to our lives. When they work, all glory is due to God. He redeems us, he provides the principles and practices, and he provides the clay that those principles and practices mold. When we see a life transformed by the twelve steps, we should direct our worship and praise to God.

Be on guard for these problems, and for others. Most people will fall into one error or another at some time (or several times). The trick is just to recognize it and take it to God in the same way as you would any other problem.

PERIODICALLY REWORK THE STEPS

Our final suggestion on step twelve is to continue working the steps yourself. In particular, we stress the importance of continuing to work steps ten, eleven, and twelve on a daily basis. But we also recommend re-working steps one through nine from time to time. Patterns of sinfulness tend to grow over time, and periodically reworking the steps will help us recognize them and address them, so that we can stay spiritually fit. It will also help us maintain credibility with our sponsees—we aren't asking them to do anything that we are not willing to continue doing ourselves.

STEP TWELVE PRACTICAL APPLICATION

Work with others. The trick here is simply to dive right in and start working with others. You'll feel overwhelmed and unqualified, but if you stick to the process outlined in this book, things will likely work themselves out. Always remember that you don't have to have the answers—you just need to know how to find them.

Ask God for help. If some of us tend to think we are unqualified, others tend to grossly overestimate their abilities. We have learned the hard way that we do not save anyone—only God does. Therefore, we should recognize our limitations and seek his aid in humility. Pray frequently for strength, discernment, wisdom, and guidance as you work with others.

Seek wise counsel from others. As we grow in experience, we tend to think that we have all the answers. This trust in self is frequently misplaced. We should admit that we are wrong, as often as not, but God in his grace has placed us in community. So, we should take advantage of this community by making it a point to seek wise counsel from others when we are not sure about how best to proceed.

Share the truth about Jesus. God has saved you and is currently working to transform you. To the extent you are seeing the fruits of that in your life, make it a point to begin to share about them with others. Tell them the truth about what God is doing for you, how grateful you are, and how they can experience the same thing.

EPILOGUE

Now the eleven disciples went to Galilee, to the mountain to which Jesus had directed them. And when they saw him they worshiped him, but some doubted. And Jesus came and said to them, "All authority in heaven and on earth has been given to me. Go therefore and make disciples of all nations, baptizing them in the name of the Father and of the Son and of the Holy Spirit, teaching them to observe all that I have commanded you. And behold, I am with you always, to the end of the age."

MATTHEW 28:16-20

It is our sincere hope that the process outlined in this book helps draw you closer to God and delivers you from the effects of compulsive sin. God has used these steps to change our lives, and we trust that he can use them to change yours.

But we also want to stress that this is only a beginning. These steps are merely a means to a larger end: to change the way we relate to God, others, and ourselves. We should not delude ourselves into thinking that because we've finished the steps, we're "fixed" and can go about our lives. Rather, because we've finished these steps, we're ready to embark on the next chapter of our lives.

God will continue to show us more. He will reveal his will to us through the Bible. He will teach us wisdom through our experiences. He will connect us with godly individuals who can provide guidance. And he will continue to make us more loving and compassionate by showing us his love and his compassion.

In other words, our work is not done—it is only beginning. Through these steps, we hope to have learned certain elementary practices and principles. The next step is to learn to apply these practices and principles to every area of our lives.

OUR STORIES

STEPHEN'S STORY

My story starts very simply: I drank and got high because I wanted to be cool. I never would have admitted it at the time, but it's as simple as that. When I got to high school I had decided my identity was going to be a punk and a skater. I started skating downtown all day Saturday and Sunday, hanging around the skate shop as much as I could, and generally being as unpleasant as possible.

I had to do more and more to fit in. Every time the ante was raised, I fearfully but willingly went along with it. When I was offered beer and marijuana I accepted. My new friends talked about porn all the time, so I started watching porn too. At sixteen I was taking hydrocodone, having sex, and drinking hard liquor. At seventeen I had tried cocaine and was using methamphetamine. At eighteen I was tired of myself and everyone around me, so I fled from Southern California to Philadelphia.

For the next few years, I stayed in a familiar cycle: I'd make some changes, things would get better for a while, but then everything would collapse.

After starting college, I was able to stay sober for about six months. During this time, I started watching pornography more frequently, often daily and for hours at a time. But when my girlfriend dumped me, I started using more heavily than ever before. Previously, my drug and alcohol consumption was light enough to be defended as me just "having fun." Now, I was getting drunk several days a week and using cocaine, ecstasy, acid, and mushrooms regularly. Within eighteen months Oxycodone, Alprazolam, and heroin were part of my routine. I started blacking out almost every time I drank. I woke up in hospitals, empty lots, and neighborhoods I'd never seen before, often with bruises, cuts or swollen knuckles. I threatened to kill myself repeatedly (I even tried once, but a good friend saved my life). My relationships weren't much better. I got a new girlfriend quickly enough and I cheated on her as frequently as I wanted to. Having gone from one relationship to another from the ages of 14 to 21, I stopped wanting a "girlfriend." I got the attention and approval I desired through sex alone and saw no need to complicate things with labels.

Things got bad enough that I resolved to get sober and started searching for solutions. I moved back and forth from Philadelphia to Austin, trying to get a handle on my life. I sought help from friends, went to psychiatrists, took all kinds of medications, got "inspired," confessed all my sins. But I kept doing all the same things over again. I had no control over my actions and the more selfish, lustful, mean, and afraid I was, the more I drank and used.

In summer of 2009, things started to change. I was working in Austin at the time, but I planned to return to Philadelphia to spend more time with a girl. But when she found out that she wasn't the only girl, things fell apart quickly. I decided there was nothing left for me in Philadelphia.

The same summer, I was opened to the twelve steps. A friend of a friend told me about an open-addiction twelve-step meeting. I had told everyone I was going to get sober, so I thought I would at least try it out. I was surprised at how much I enjoyed the meetings. I found a sponsor within a couple weeks (although not before I found a new girlfriend) and began to work the steps.

At this point in my life, I had never given spiritual matters serious consideration. Aside from reading a few pages of the Bible and a few pages of the Koran, I had not devoted any time to learning about religion. When I was 17, my girlfriend was badly injured in a car crash. That night I prayed for the first time, asking God to help her. When she got out of the hospital a few hours later, I decided I believed in God. Unfortunately, that was as far as my beliefs went. Aside from superficial and fearful prayer, and a burdensome feeling that God was punishing me, I didn't have a spiritual life. However, when my sponsor informed me that I needed a relationship with God to stay sober, I didn't resist. The concept made sense to me and I took his suggestions as he encouraged me to pray, meditate, and complete the rest of the twelve steps.

Slowly, things started to change. I stopped taking the sedatives I had convinced myself I needed to "help me sleep." My girlfriend and I parted ways. I began to want to help other alcoholics who were struggling, and so I became very involved in twelve-step work: I went to at least a meeting every day, sponsored several guys, started a beginners meeting, and regularly co-chaired a meeting at a detox center. At 18 months of sobriety, after regularly watching pornography for about 10 years, I stopped looking at porn altogether, something I thought impossible. My attitude slowly changed as well. I became grateful for my new life and interested in God. I prayed regularly and gained new awareness of my character flaws. God was changing me, though at the time I didn't realize how radical a change He was planning.

It wasn't long before I let all of this go to my head. I became brash, legalistic, and condescending on spiritual matters. I had changed, so why couldn't everyone else? I had no understanding of grace: either God's grace for me, or the grace I ought to have with others. I confidently barked about God and spiritual law and put down anyone and everyone who didn't see things my way. I thought I'd changed myself, and so I saw no reason to be humble. It was years before this attitude wore off.

During this time, I met Megan, the woman who would eventually become my wife.

Although I was "in love" with her, I had no ability to love her, in the Christian sense of the term: I didn't know how to sacrifice, or be patient or honest. I was still very much self-interested and without God in our relationship, it crumbled in a matter of months.

Although the deterioration of this relationship was painful, it eventually brought me to a place of clarity. Sex and relationships were idols I had clung to longer than all the others. I wanted love and companionship, but I didn't want to put in the effort to cultivate those things or accept the responsibility that went with them, so I settled for sex and attention. I had always thought of sex selfishly and obsessively: I wanted to have as much as I could, and didn't always care about the consequences. In relationships, even when I was physically faithful, I lusted after and had emotionally charged relationships with other women. When the thought first occurred to me that I shouldn't have sex again until I was married, I immediately rejected it and tried to think of a way around it. The struggle was short lived and when I accepted this proposition, I felt immediately and physically relieved. It was as though a weight had been lifted, and I don't just mean that figuratively: I felt lighter. Sex had always been a burden in my life, and I assumed it always would be, but I was suddenly and unexpectedly free. It was not until much later that I realized that this was the last obstacle standing in the way of accepting Christ. I was like the woman at the well who couldn't bear to be alone: only the living water of Christ was a sufficient substitute.

I had become more and more interested in Christ over the previous year, but this change allowed me to take spiritual matters more seriously. A friend took me to church and I read the Gospels. Jesus impressed and surprised me and I suddenly wondered if I had misjudged Christianity. I prayed to understand Christ and what he meant to my life. I wanted to know Christ so badly, but I thought I never would. I tried to make peace with the idea that Christianity wasn't for me, but one night a great wave of emotion came over me and all my prayers were answered: for a moment, I understood this Jesus and what he came to Earth for. Then it subsided. Within a few weeks, the overwhelming passion I felt that night was replaced by a much calmer conviction that Christ was who he said he was: the Way, the Truth, and the Life.

Since that time, I have been shaped by the Holy Spirit. However, I haven't always accepted these changes gracefully. As an introvert and misanthrope, being part of a church community has been exceptionally difficult for me. It was nearly a year before I could even admit that being part of a church is integral to Christian life. (Although I am very involved with church today, it continues to be a struggle.) Similarly, coming to believe in the exclusivity of the gospel and the inerrancy of scripture was a rocky road. The idea that there is only one way offends my contemporary sensibilities.

However, the more I read scripture and pray, the more convicted I become that Christ is the only true hope for the lost and that the Bible is God's word: perfect even when I don't understand it—or don't like it.

A few months after my breakup with Megan, I had an unexpected opportunity to reconnect with her. I was scared about going down this path again, but I prayed about it and felt encouraged to give it another chance. I explained to her that I had come to Christ and how it had changed my view of sex and relationships. Although it was difficult and not perfect, we practiced chastity and focused more on the spiritual than the physical in our relationship. We started praying and going to church together and eventually she joined a Bible study. Several months later she was saved. About a year after that we were married. Although marriage is very challenging, my transformation from an unfaithful lecher incapable of even being in an exclusive relationship to a faithful husband whose guide is the Gospel is indeed a miraculous one.

Today, my life bears little resemblance to my life before sobriety, or before I knew Christ. Through twelve-step fellowships, I have learned about service and responsibility. Through church life, I have learned about community, understanding, and commitment to biblical truth. Through marriage I have learned about persistence, faithfulness, and self-sacrifice. In my daily life, I am constantly blessed with opportunities to grow: sometimes I take them and sometimes I insist on my way. Although I still struggle with lust, resentment, and selfishness, my struggles are different today because I want to follow God's will for me, even when I fail to do so. And when I do fall short, I don't have to take the burden on my own shoulders: I know Christ's sacrifice has paid the cost of all my sins, no matter how heavy. Over time and through God's grace, I have been blessed with a new identity in Jesus Christ.

CHRISTINA'S STORY

I was born into a typical family on a small farm in North Carolina. My parents both worked full-time jobs, we went to church, and we prayed before meals. But my father was distant—and I longed for his approval. My mother and I were close, and yet I felt very different from her. I palled around with my brother, but he could be harsh towards me. I was an emotional kid, but I quickly learned that I was supposed to keep my issues to myself.

For as long as I can remember, I've been anxious, and I learned how to compensate. I tried to soothe myself with music, movies, poetry, and food. I would check out mentally and I spent lots of time in my imagination—where no one could hurt me, disappoint me, or not love me.

When I was eight, my grandmother decided I should be baptized. She also began to pray for my salvation, but those prayers would not be answered for 17 years.

Three years later, my parents divorced. My dad and brother stayed in North Carolina, but my mom and I moved to south Texas. I was heartbroken. But I also met my mother's family and was embraced by them. I, in turn, began to embrace my "new identity": Mexican-American. I "finally" knew who I was and where I belonged.

That was the first of many new identities.

When I was 14, I got my first boyfriend and began acting out behind my mom's back. My first semester of high school I slacked off and failed my courses, and then quickly bounced back. Next semester I had all A's. This kind of up and down behavior would be a pattern for many years to come. I came into my next identity: "smart girl."

At age 16, I drank my first drink and I felt free. I seemed to come alive and I could be the care-free and crazy girl I longed to be in my real life. This was my first introduction to a new way I could escape reality.

I went off to college at a top-tier university. I did well my first semester, and even better the next. I couldn't wait to show off this new version of myself to my dad.

But that year, my dad passed away suddenly from a massive heart attack. My whole world got flipped upside down, and something changed in my heart. I began to party and drink heavily. I was devastated, but I also felt relieved that I no longer had to "live up to" my dad's standards.

So, I started my third semester partying and skipping class. Again, my academics began to suffer, and again I bounced back to graduate on time and get a job. My relationship ended and so I swore off drinking and impurity. I was moving on, I thought. But I was also depressed, lonely, and began to binge eat. I traded one addiction for another. And I began to find my identity in my work.

Around this time, I also started going to church with a friend. Here, everything was different. I felt safe and near to God in the worship services. But when I came back home, hopelessness returned. And the binge-eating continued. My spiritual life was very compartmentalized.

Eventually, I found a twelve-step fellowship for binge-eating and began attending meetings. I was frustrated at the idea that I might be powerless over food. I was also frustrated that their definition of "Higher Power" was so loose. Yet I would still go.

Around this time, I also joined a small group at church and we started reading the

Bible together. It was like nails on a chalkboard for me. I heard the preachers talk about the importance of the Word of God so I began to pray that I would have a love for it. One Monday, my group came to check out Recovery—a Christ-centered twelve-step program at my church. People here were real and honest and they were boldly proclaiming their need for Jesus. The atmosphere was authentic and captivating and I had never experienced church like this.

Several months went by and one night, amidst the pain of another breakup, I cried out to God. I knelt down beside my bed and told him, "I'll do anything you ask me, I'll be powerless to whatever you want. I know you're the answer. Help me." And in an instant, he came to me and answered me. The words of Psalm 34 are my words. "I cried out to the Lord and he answered me and delivered me from all my fears."

I stepped out in faith and obedience, shaking and afraid. But my fear could no longer hold me back—I had encountered the living God and His power was irresistible and wooing, even in the dark times.

I found a sponsor and began to work the steps. I began to see victory over my binge-eating, but my drinking began to pick back up. One night I was out with my coworkers, and as one drink turned into four, I soon found myself drunk. But something had changed in me

The next morning, I woke up full of regret, but for the first time I was sorry to God for what I'd done. I had a new heart. I would come to realize that no one can serve two masters. I couldn't deny my alcoholism any longer.

I began to attend another twelve-step fellowship geared towards substance abuse, and quickly got swept up in the community. I began to learn how to live without alcohol. I was scared and undisciplined, but I was learning to rely on God, to ask for help from others, to serve others when I felt self-pity, and to give thanks in all circumstances. God began to transform the way I related to him, to others, and to myself. He also taught me steadfastness, even in the midst of suffering. I went through another bout of depression, but he taught me how to rely upon him for hope, even when things seemed hopeless.

I have spent a lot of my life wishing I had a different story, a different personality, wishing I were prettier, smarter, more talented, skinnier, anything but "me." My walk with Christ has been a constant chipping away through all the layers of delusion and dissatisfaction to show me that I was made by him and made for him. I'm unique and different, but different is not bad. He made me special and precious. I'm fearfully and wonderfully made in His image and what he has made and what he has called good no one and no thing can call otherwise.

My mom recently told me that I always followed the rules—as long as I understood them. I've learned that godly obedience is different from this: godly obedience follows directions even when it doesn't understand because the authority can be trusted.

Today I cherish my story because it is how God brought me to himself. He has redeemed so much in my life. He gave me a big, vibrant, loving spiritual family. He gave me a love for the Bible that I didn't have. He gave me healing from grief with my dad. He gave me purity and sobriety and a love to serve and obey him. He gave me the boldness to move out of a life of comfort and fear into adventure. He gave me a childlike spirit and silliness and freedom to be me.

Today I am a different person. I am every day changing into the person he made me to be.

PHIL'S STORY

By the time I was a sophomore in high school, I had been drinking and getting high for five years.

It started as an attempt to fit in with older, cooler guys, but it turned out I found it quite enjoyable. It not only made me happy and eased my adolescent awkwardness, it also gave me an identity and a sense of belonging. I continued until I was getting high almost every day and couldn't turn down a drink or a drug—no matter the consequences.

I was forced to attend a twelve-step meeting here and there, but I never participated and tried my best to avoid talking to anyone. Still, I saw that these people drank and used drugs the way I did, but were sober—and more importantly, happy.

I, on the other hand, was definitely not happy. While things seemed okay on the outside, I was miserable. I got good grades and played sports, but I didn't know who I was—my identity and purpose were wrapped up in mindless substance abuse. My life was marked by shame, fear, loneliness, envy, discontent, dishonesty, and a desire to escape the unpleasantness of reality.

After getting caught drunk at school, I decided to give sobriety a shot. I wanted to be successful, have loving relationships, and live with integrity. I was graced with the foresight to see that the current way I was living wouldn't get me there.

I went back to the happy people in the twelve-step meetings and asked for help. I was immediately taken in and invited to participate in coffee after the meeting and the sober party that was going on that weekend. It was a relief to be accepted by these people, and I was hopeful that I would be able to find whatever it was that they had.

They told me if I wanted what they had, I needed to get a sponsor and work the steps. It took another month of relapses before I finally took that advice.

I didn't know where to start. I didn't know a thing about God or what he would want from me. But I was told that this was okay, as long as I was willing to try. When I took the simple suggestions my sponsor offered, I found the desire to drink and get high lifted. Things started to improve.

Eight months later, I was still stalling on my fourth step. I was chasing relationships with girls instead of a relationship with God. I prioritized the comfort of romantic intimacy over the vulnerability and exposure of doing my inventory. I relapsed again and felt more hopeless than ever.

While I was afraid of the possibility of never being able to achieve lasting sobriety, I focused on the fact that it was working for other people. I was given new willingness and re-committed to working the steps. Through the steps, I began to build a relationship with God, resulting in lasting sobriety.

But it wasn't long before my compulsive nature started showing up in other areas of my life. I began seeking comfort in romantic relationships, sex, pornography, success at school and work, materialism, food, video games, isolation, and tobacco use. These habits never brought me as low as my substance abuse, but they all led me down the same cycle of relief, remorse and emptiness.

I also stopped working with a sponsor. I thought I had my spiritual life under control—that I was a teacher, not a student. I grew dangerously proud and closed-minded in my spiritual walk.

In my seventh year of sobriety I found myself at a new bottom as an unhealthy relationship came to an end. I was face-to-face with my own brokenness once again. I knew that if I didn't recommit to my recovery program that I was likely to relapse. My fear gave me a greater willingness. I found a new sponsor, went through the steps again, and started taking suggestions that leveled my pride. Part of me felt that I had too much "time" to call my sponsor every day, but doing so forced me to confront my pride and really cultivated a relationship between us built on trust and vulnerability.

It was around this time that my relationship with God started to change.

During the first seven years of sobriety, I wanted God to do a lot for me, but I wasn't really willing to do much for Him. I was living for myself, seeking pleasure and comfort in all kinds of worldly things. There were a few times when I would feel really broken and see the futility of my way of life, but they were short lived and I would find worldly successes to distract me from my brokenness.

Through working with my sponsor, I became convinced that a relationship with God had to be the most important thing in my life. I knew that nothing else would break the cycle of selfishness that I was living in. However, I also began to realize my powerlessness. I wanted to serve God, but I found myself succumbing to the world. For the next two years, I struggled with resisting worldly temptations that I now knew conflicted with my desire to grow in faith and usefulness to God.

In the midst of this struggle, God began to open my eyes to the truth about Jesus. Several of my close friends in recovery became Christians and started to talk to me about Christ.

Up to this point I had always resisted organized religion. In fact, I was somewhat offended by it and quite outspoken in my distaste. I didn't grow up with it and since I first got sober I had believed that any conception of God was fine and nobody had any authority to say otherwise. I didn't particularly care for their message.

But it was hard to ignore that their lives were being changed. They seemed to be getting beyond the temptations of the world and making huge leaps of growth in their faith. I could see that nothing was more important to them than their relationship with God, not just ideally but functionally—in the way they were living. It really seemed like they were onto something.

Eventually, I began to break. Fueled by pride and fear of the unknown, I fought their efforts for months. But soon I had a change of heart and became willing to give this gospel they talked about an honest appraisal. I started attending church with these patient friends and reading through some apologetic literature with them, trying to set aside my prejudices.

I began to realize that I was resisting the truth about Christ because I was afraid of the implications it would have on my life. My own conception of God enabled me to behave however I wanted. When I wanted to engage in a behavior that was "ungodly", I would just change my beliefs about what godly was. I couldn't do that with Jesus. He is who he is, regardless of what I want him to be.

As I began to admit that my ideas about God were not grounded in absolute truth, I continued to learn more about Jesus. More importantly, I began to ask God to help me believe in Jesus if all this was indeed real. Then, one night as I was reading in bed I was struck by the realization that I really did believe in the Jesus of the bible: that he was divine and that his death on the cross had paid for all my sins. I knew that this would change my world, but I was now much more excited about knowing God as he is than I was afraid of losing myself. With my newfound faith, I felt armed with a greater sense of purpose and the strength to resist the temptations that I had struggled with so much in the past few years. It wasn't so much that temptation was absent, but rather that the certainty of God's presence in my life enabled me to seek pleasure and comfort in Him.

I have often reflected on this time and wondered how someone so rebellious, closed-minded, and proud could come to believe in Christ. How did I become willing to explore? How did I ever admit that I could be wrong? Why did I keep asking questions and stick around even when I was confused, overwhelmed and afraid? I can't explain how these barriers were surmounted and it certainly had nothing to do with me. The only explanation I have is that Jesus continued to seek me, softening my heart and drawing me near.

I have seen so much growth in the two years since my conversion. God has reshaped my worldview and redeemed some of the most broken parts of my life. He has taken me to a new job in a new city and given me a new fellowship of believers to worship and serve with. I have found a recovery fellowship as well and continue to find guidance and accountability in the twelve steps. I have been given the opportunity to mend relationships with my family that had become distant in my years away from home. I have been blessed to marry my best friend who constantly challenges me to remain faithful to the god who has faithfully pursued me. In the midst of all of this change I have seen my faith grow as I witness the constancy of God and how he provides for me in feast and in famine.

ROBERT'S STORY

They let me out of my jail cell at about 1 PM. I'd been arrested the night before for public intoxication. According to the arrest report, I'd attacked the driver of the private bus that had been hired by the friends of the groom whose bachelor party I had crashed. The driver pulled the bus over, threw me out, and called the cops.

I don't remember much about that night, except that I refused to answer any questions, including giving them my name. So, they took away my clothes, put me on suicide watch, and gave me one of those examination gowns you sometimes get at the hospital to spend the night in.

The next afternoon I got my clothes back, stiff with alcohol and dirt. The cab driver who took me home asked if I'd just gotten out of jail. I said yes, and told him I didn't know what to do next. He didn't respond.

When I got home I told my brother what had happened. He said he figured, and had already found my mug shot online. I sat on the same couch where I'd started drinking the night before. I knew getting arrested would have consequences that I should start mitigating, but I didn't even feel like coming up with a plan. I just knew I needed help.

I went to my doctor first. He said I had anxiety and needed help. So, he referred me to a therapist. Within five minutes, she prescribed five twelve-step meetings in the week before she saw me again. She saved my life.

These meetings brought me back to a bar where a bunch of disreputable looking men had decided to start a meeting. They talked about honor and purpose and honesty, and above all, they talked about being given a second chance to pursue those things only because of the kindness and mercy of the all-powerful God of the universe.

These men—pimps, felons, and possibly worse—seemed to be sober and free. What struck me about these men was their brutal honesty, the nature of their fellowship, and the fact that they gave the credit for their recovery to God working through the steps—not the steps themselves.

So, I kept coming back and I worked the steps (to the best of my ability).

My arrest shattered my self-image, and I was desperate to experience the freedom these men had, so I poured myself into being brutally honest and working the steps well.

I can't really remember what happened over the next few months. My memory of my early sobriety is fuzzy. What I do remember doing is the daily disciplines my sponsor and friends told me to do: make my bed every morning, pray, read twelve-step literature, talk to other alcoholics, go to a meeting, and call my sponsor.

Eventually, a friend at this meeting invited me to church.

And for reasons I can't explain, I added to my list of spiritual disciplines: reading or thinking or talking about whether Jesus actually lived, died, and was resurrected. A lot of resources led me to conclude that he was who he said he was. So, logically, I was baptized and became a member at that church later that year.

Since then, things have become much clearer. My previous paths to comfort—alcohol, pornography, masturbation—were closed. New paths opened: prayer, community, reading the Bible.

Dedication to these new paths saved me from loneliness and purposelessness. Whereas before my intimacy with women was primarily drunk, physical, instantly unsatisfying and shame-inducing, now I have found a relationship with a woman in which I find greater satisfaction every minute than in the total of all of my previous relationships because now I have been given the ability to be emotionally and spiritually intimate with another person.

Whereas before I had never desired to work hard at anything, thinking that success would be natural and an effortless result of my natural abilities, now I find myself striving for little or no compensation at seemingly impossible work. I am content with the certainty that because I have committed these pursuits to God there is an eternal weight of glory saved up for me in the next life even if nothing should come of them in this one.

Whereas before I had been ruled by resentment and anger towards my earthly parents, now I am ruled by my Heavenly Father, the King of love, who commands me to honor my parents at the same time that he gives me the willingness and ability to do it as well as unrelenting pardon when I fail.

I will shortly reach three years of sobriety. There have been times throughout these three years when I tell God that I would be satisfied with my life even if it were never to get any better. Then my circumstances do get better, and I tell him again.

My story is not unique; I have seen the same in the lives of my friends who have also been desperate for help, inquired of Jesus honestly, and committed themselves to living out what seems to be true. I am grateful to believe that it is the natural product of a system designed by a perfect, merciful, and loving God to give life to those who want it.

ALEX'S STORY

I was first exposed to pornography at 11 while at a friend's house. I felt awful physically afterward, but I also wanted to experience it again. A few years later, my family got the Internet and I quickly learned I could access all of the pornography I wanted right in my own home. I didn't think of it this way at the time, but by 16 I was an addict.

I began to live in fear. I grew up in a Christian home, went to church every Sunday and Wednesday, and would have been considered a "fine young man" by just about anyone in town. Because of this, I lived a double life. I wanted to keep my golden boy image, but I was crumbling inside and afraid of being found out.

I resolved to fix myself. I daily prayed for God to let me win the battle over temptation, and I daily slipped back into my slavery to pornography. I realize now that I had not grasped one of the simplest truths of the gospel—God transforms my life, not me. By the time I went off to college, I was still a slave to my sin and I had still not told anyone. I was lonely and isolated, in a bad place and things were getting worse.

But eventually God gave me a chance to confess my sin to a Bible-study leader, and he placed me in a community that began to teach me what it was like to surrender all of myself to God and let him change me.

For the next ten years I could see that God was changing me, but I also was still falling into old patterns. Despite my freedom in Christ, I was giving sin a foothold in my life. Paul's experience of our competing natures (in Romans 7:21-25) described my life to a T. And like Paul, I felt wretched. I had experienced the fullness of God's grace and mercy, and yet regularly chose to turn my back on him.

Then came a turning point. A close friend who knew about my struggle with pornography encouraged me to attend a recovery meeting. I didn't want to go, but I told him I would, so like a good "golden boy," I did. At my first meeting, I met the man who would become my sponsor.

God used him to guide me through the twelve steps and point me towards Christ. Working through the steps was the first time that I had looked that deep into my sin as well as all the rest of my life. It exposed underlying desires and sin issues that affected every area of my life, especially my struggle with pornography. This was hard to admit, but it was also very freeing to see my heart for what it was, especially in light of the gospel.

God continues to show me that His work in me is not finished. I didn't go through the steps just to come out clean and fixed for the rest of my life. Temptation is not gone and Paul's description of my competing natures is still apt. But God has shown me his grace, and he continues to show me my need for him.

"Who will deliver me from this body of death? Thanks be to God through Jesus Christ our Lord!"

APPENDIX A
THE GOSPEL

What is the Gospel? **The Gospel is the good news that God has acted decisively in history to defeat evil and reconcile sinful humanity to himself through the life, death, and resurrection of his son, Jesus Christ.** That is a dense statement, so it helps to explain it in a simple framework. One such framework is the "Creation, Fall, Redemption, Consummation" paradigm. This approach grounds the solution in an understanding of the problem, while also giving us an easy-to-follow structure when we are explaining it to others.

CREATION

Human beings are fundamentally good creatures—because we are made in the image of God—and fundamentally dependent creatures—because we are made to live in fellowship with, obedience to, and reliance upon him. Our lives have no meaning apart from fellowship with him, and our lives have no purpose apart from extending his kingdom across the earth. Adam and Eve have only two things to do in the garden: enjoy the presence of God and be fruitful and subdue the earth, filling it with God's image bearers.[62]

God's order for the creation is that humans are designed for a vertical relationship with God, working in unity and living in fellowship with one another in pursuit of the common goal of worshiping and glorifying him through good works.[63] Because this is how we are designed to function, this is the only way for us to be truly content.

FALL

The biblical storyline is that we are glorious creatures gone tragically bad. Three chapters into the Bible, humans decide to reject God's order. Enticed by a lack of trust in God and a desire to be like God (Genesis 3:1-7), humans set themselves up over and against God, both in Eden and today. What seems like an innocuous infraction—eating a fruit—was in fact an act of rebellion, an attempt to depose God from the throne of the universe and the throne of our hearts, and run things to suit ourselves. It is the dethroning of God.

This act of rebellion has two primary results. The first is spiritual death. Engaged in the futile task of finding real purpose and meaning apart from God, we engage in all

---

[62] *Cf.* Genesis 1:28.
[63] *Cf.* Ephesians 2:10.

manner of idolatry and unrighteousness, tarnishing (but never erasing) God's image inside us and enslaving ourselves to the power of sin and death. Our will is trapped, our hearts are darkened, and our thinking becomes futile.[64]

The second is physical death. God makes good on his statement that the price of eating the fruit is death. He drives them out of Eden (Genesis 3:22-24), and condemns them to return to dust apart from the tree of life (Genesis 3:19). The effects of this corruption spread outward to the rest of the creation (Genesis 3:17-19), which is subjected to futility and put in bondage to corruption.[65]

But even amid his wrath and just condemnation, God also shows his mercy and love for Adam and Eve, making clothes for them before driving them out into the world (Genesis 3:21). The tension between these two thematic elements—God's wrath and justice, on the one hand, and his mercy and love, on the other—continues to mount throughout the rest of the Old Testament.

REDEMPTION

Yet from the beginning, God promises to resolve this tension and redeem the whole creation from the toxic effects of sin. This resolution is finally affected by the work of Jesus Christ.

Because we could not come to him, God came to us. The Creator God moved into the created order, not to condemn it, but to save it.[66] He became a human being, a first-century Jewish craftsman, probably around five feet tall and about 130 pounds, named Yeshua, or in English, Joshua or Jesus. He traveled around Palestine as an itinerant teacher speaking in parables, healing the sick, feeding the hungry, comforting the brokenhearted, and challenging corruption, showing us not only who God is, but also what humans are supposed to be.

Jesus completes his vocation to redeem humanity at the cross. He "was delivered up for our trespasses and raised for our justification." (Romans 4:25). He delivered us from our trespasses in that he took our sins upon himself,[67] the "record of debt that stood against us with its legal demands," and "nail[ed] it to the cross," (Colossians 2:14). He was raised for our justification in that he rose from the dead as the firstborn of a new creation (1 Corinthians 15:20-23), a new Adam (Romans 5:12-21), offering to effect a cosmic substitution: by the grace of God, his righteous life can be exchanged for our sinful lives through our faith in him,[68] not based on our deeds but in faith

---

[64] *Cf.* Romans 1:21-23.
[65] *Cf.* Romans 8:19-21.
[66] *Cf.* John 3:16-17.
[67] *Cf.* 2 Corinthians 5:21; Isaiah 53:3-11.
[68] *See* John 3:16; Romans 3:22; Galatians 2:16; Ephesians 2:4-9.

in God's deeds: "[f]or all have sinned and fall short of the glory of God, and all are justified by his grace as a gift, through the redemption that is in Christ Jesus … to be received by faith" (Romans 3:23-24). At the cross, God's justice and his mercy meet, he is able to be both just, *i.e.*, satisfying the demands of God's law, and justifier, *i.e.*, the God who declares guilty sinners righteous.[69] In short, "if anyone is in Christ, he is a new creation" (2 Corinthians 5:17).

CONSUMMATION

The cross marks the decisive moment in human history. On the one hand, it is the place where Christ's redeeming work is finished.[70] On the other, it is only the beginning of his contested reign, which will only come to an end when he has destroyed all ungodly dominion, authority, and power and put all enemies under his feet—the last enemy being death—before handing his kingdom over to his father.[71] We live in between those two events, and that "already-but-not-yet kingdom" is breaking its way into our world.

This kingdom **already** exists as a present spiritual kingdom within the hearts of believers, marked by the "down payment" of the Holy Spirit dwelling within us,[72] thereby being ransomed from spiritual slavery and receiving heavenly wisdom,[73] but **not yet** as a physical kingdom through a new heaven and a new earth, marked by God himself returning to dwell among us here on earth.[74]

Thus, Christians are brought forth as new creations in anticipation of the eventual renewal of the whole created order to fulfill the purpose of humanity in extending God's kingdom across the earth. They are saved, but saved for a purpose. God has called Christians out of darkness into light so that they might be light to others.[75] Simply put, we are called to consummate our redemption by "working out"—through the power of God who works in us "to will and act in order to fulfill his good purpose"—what Christ has already accomplished (Philippians 2:12-13).

CONCLUSION

The gospel, then, is the message about how Christ ties up all the loose ends created by the fall. Whereas the fall brings spiritual death through slavery to sin, Christ brings spiritual life by ransoming us from sin's power over us. Whereas the fall

---

[69] *Cf.* Romans 3:26.
[70] *Cf.* John 19:30.
[71] *Cf.* 1 Corinthians 15:24-28.
[72] *Cf.* Luke 17:20-21; Ephesians 1:14-16; 2 Corinthians 1:22.
[73] *Cf.* Ephesians 1:7, 17-18.
[74] *Cf.* Revelation 21:1-3.
[75] *Cf.* 1 Peter 2:9, Matthew 5:14-16.

brings physical death through alienation from God, Christ brings physical life by reconciling us to God while filling us with the Holy Spirit. Having been brought back to God and called into his redemptive mission, we find purpose and meaning again, and thereby receive true contentment in service to the Creator rather than the creation. Thus, scripture speaks of the gospel in at least five ways:

The gospel of Christ. The good news of salvation through the person and work of Jesus Christ.[76]

The gospel of the grace of God. The good news of salvation by grace through faith, not merit.[77]

The gospel of the kingdom. The good news that God will establish his kingdom on earth.[78]

The gospel of peace. The good news that salvation in Christ brings peace—with God and with others.[79]

The everlasting gospel. The good news about revering, glorifying, and worshiping God properly.[80]

This is good news indeed!

---

[76] *See* Mark 1:1; 1 Corinthians 9:2; Romans 1:9.
[77] *See* Acts 20:24.
[78] *See* Matthew 4:23, 9:35, 24:14.
[79] *See* Ephesians 6:15
[80] *See* Revelation 14:6.

APPENDIX B
INVENTORIES

Download a full-page version of the inventories at providenceaustin.com/inventories

BASIC INVENTORY

WHO/WHAT	WHICH NATURAL DESIRE WAS THREATENED OR AT STAKE?		MY PART		GOSPEL TRUTHS
Briefly describe the resentment, fear, sin, or relationship	Power	*How does this affect my desire for power over other people?*	Selfish	*How did I fail to consider others?*	*What aspects of God's truth, if believed more fully, would help address this situation (indicatives, not imperatives)*
	Approval	*How does this affect my desire for approval or affirmation (including respect)?*	Dishonest	*What was I hiding or unwilling to admit?*	
	Comfort	*How does this affect my desire for comfort or pleasure?*	Self-Seeking	*How was I trying to glorify myself?*	
	Security	*How does this affect my desire for security and control over circumstances?*	Afraid	*What was I afraid to lose?*	
	Power		Selfish		
	Approval		Dishonest		
	Comfort		Self-Seeking		
	Security		Afraid		
	Power		Selfish		
	Approval		Dishonest		
	Comfort		Self-Seeking		
	Security		Afraid		
	Power		Selfish		
	Approval		Dishonest		
	Comfort		Self-Seeking		
	Security		Afraid		

DETAILED INVENTORY

SIN	WHICH NATURAL DESIRE WAS THREATENED OR AT STAKE?		MY PART (HOW WAS I …)		GOSPEL TRUTHS
Briefly describe the resentment, fear, sin, or relationship	**Power**	*Power, influence, control over others*	**Unloving**	*Inconsiderate, selfish, self-seeking*	*What aspects of God's truth, if believed more fully, would help address this sin (indicatives, not imperatives)*
			Bitter	*Hateful, angry, discontent*	
	Approval	*Respect, approval, admiration*	**Combative**	*Attacking others, in word/thought*	
			Vengeful	*Seeking vengeance or vindication*	
	Comfort	*Comfort, ease, pleasure, contentment*	**Harsh**	*Unmerciful, unkind, harsh, judgmental*	
			Dishonest	*Deceitful, afraid to admit truth, hiding*	
	Security	*Security, control over circumstances*	**Doubting**	*Failing to trust God and his provision*	
			Proud	*Considering yourself more important than others*	
	Power		**Unloving**		
			Bitter		
	Approval		**Combative**		
			Vengeful		
	Comfort		**Harsh**		
			Dishonest		
	Security		**Doubting**		
			Proud		
	Power		**Unloving**		
			Bitter		
	Approval		**Combative**		
			Vengeful		
	Comfort		**Harsh**		
			Dishonest		
	Security		**Afraid**		
			Proud		
	Power		**Unloving**		
			Bitter		
	Approval		**Combative**		
			Vengeful		
	Comfort		**Harsh**		
			Dishonest		
	Security		**Doubting**		
			Proud		

www.ingramcontent.com/pod-product-compliance
Lightning Source LLC
Chambersburg PA
CBHW061127100726
47911CB00013B/704